DANGEROUS LOVE

PAT BALLARD

PEARLSONG PRESS
NASHVILLE, TN

Pearlsong Press
P.O. Box 58065
Nashville, TN 37205
www.pearlsong.com
www.pearlsongpress.com

Original trade paperback ISBN: 9781597190534
Ebook ISBN: 9781597190541

Book & cover design by Zelda Pudding
Cover art © Kheng Guan Toh—Fotolia.com

Library of Congress Cataloging-in-Publication data

Ballard, Pat (Patricia F.)
  Dangerous love / Pat Ballard.
      p. cm.
  ISBN 978-1-59719-053-4 (original trade pbk.: alk. paper)— ISBN 978-1-59719-054-1 (ebook)
  1. Laboratory technicians—Fiction. 2. Overweight women—Fiction. 3. Weight loss preparations—Fiction. 4. Fraud in science—Fiction. 5. Los Angeles (Calif.) Police Dept.—Officials and employees—Fiction. 6. Medical fiction. I. Title.

PS3552.A4664D366 2011
813'.54—dc22

                                              2011016885

DEDICATED TO MY HUSBAND, JOE,
WHO GAVE ME THE IDEA FOR THIS BOOK.

CHAPTER 1

Ava Manning blinked her eyes, squinted and leaned closer to the computer screen. The results she saw on the spreadsheet didn't match the results she'd seen a week ago. Yet it was supposed to be the same research database that Professor James Lutz had allowed her and her fellow lab technician, Mike Campbell, to observe when he'd first presented it.

While getting her degree as a scientific researcher, Ava worked as a lab technician at a large pharmaceutical company, Cloneall Drugs, Inc. The researchers' main goal at Cloneall Drugs was to find data to prove that obesity was a stand-alone cause of disease and premature death. The movers and shakers at Cloneall Drugs, Inc. were specifically dedicated to developing a drug that would annihilate obesity. Especially William Turnball, the owner and CEO. It was a known fact that William Turnball detested anyone who had one extra pound on them. In a recent interview, when asked what he considered overweight for a woman, he answered with a smirk on his tanned, handsome face, "Anything over a size zero."

Ava's interest in Cloneall Drugs, and the reason she wanted her position with the company, was in hopes that the research would actually turn up the opposite result. She longed for data that would show without a shadow of a doubt that obesity of and by itself did not cause adverse health problems or premature death. She knew research already existed to that effect, but she wanted more. She wanted to see it unfold with her own eyes. She wanted to be a part of the unfolding of such groundbreaking research. And she wanted to be able to get that information to the entire world.

She'd fought her weight all her life. Had gone on every fad diet that came along, only to gain back any weight she lost. She'd usually gain back a few pounds more than she'd weighed when she started.

In college she'd become aware of all the eating disorders the young women had developed. Being around that many women at once, she'd been amazed at how many of them seemed to actually hate their bodies. She'd been alarmed at the great extent they would go to in order to conform to the societal ideal of what a woman should look like.

That had been a wakeup call for Ava. She'd decided that she simply would not waste her precious brainpower and energy on trying to look like some of the emaciated supermodels splashed on television, big screens, and most of the magazines on the newsstands. So she used all her physical and mental energies to pursue her education and ready herself for the position she had at Cloneall Drugs, Inc. so she could help make a difference in the world of women of all ages everywhere.

She thought she was witnessing her chance to do that last week when she'd seen the results of Professor Lutz's 4,600 male/female blind study, which had been carried out over the past 10 years. But the numbers before her now showed something entirely different. They showed the exact opposite of what she had seen in the previous data. She was looking at numbers showing that a BMI (Body Mass Index) of over 25 rapidly decreased the quality of health in both males and females, independent of any other factors like diabetes, hypertension, or high cholesterol.

Ava suddenly felt as if she were in the Twilight Zone. She cautiously glanced around the lab. She was in the right place. Ted, Lisa and Mike all sat with their eyes glued to their computer screens.

Mike was the only other technician that Professor Lutz had allowed to see the original study. Had he noticed the difference? As she watched him, Mike raised his eyes to hers. She could tell by the look on his face that he had noticed the data were different.

As she and Mike looked at each other, Professor Lutz walked into the room. Mike gave a quick shake of his head, warning Ava not to say anything, then mouthed the word "Later."

"Good morning, ladies and gentlemen," Professor Lutz said. "I see you've discovered the data I uploaded onto all your computers. These are some very exciting times! This research will prove once and for all that being just a little overweight is a very bad, unhealthy thing. Mr. Turnball will be extremely happy with these findings." His glance skirted from Mike to Ava. "Does anyone have any questions about the data?" he asked.

Ava could almost feel him fishing to see if she or Mike had noticed the difference, or if they dared to challenge him.

"Mike," he probed, "how do you feel about this study?"

"The numbers are here, Professor Lutz. You can't argue with numbers like these," Mike said, again casting a warning glance at Ava.

"And you, Ava? Are you happy with what you see?" The professor persisted.

"What's not to be happy about, Professor? These numbers are perfect to back up the development of a new drug to combat obesity. You should be very happy with the outcome of your research." *Or the rigging of said research*, she wanted to add.

"Very good!" Professor Lutz said, satisfied that he had cooperation of his two lead technicians. "Now I'm off to have a meeting with Mr. Turnball and give him the good news, then I'll be out of town for a couple of weeks. Continue with your projects and I'll see you when I get back."

"What's going on?" Ava asked Mike as soon as they were sure Professor Lutz was gone.

"I'm not sure. Maybe we misunderstood the data we saw last week," Mike answered.

"It's not even close to what we saw last week!" Ava hissed. "The data we saw last week showed obesity had absolutely no negative association with health. Do you think he changed the numbers?"

"Ava! You can't even think that!" Mike said, glancing around to see if any of the other technicians were listening to them. "We can't prove what we saw last week, so there's absolutely no reason to lose our jobs over it! It's practically unheard of for researchers to change or modify data! And accusing one of doing it is even more unheard of. You just need to forget about this and let it drop."

"Mike, I'm not training to be a scientist so I can be a part of bogus research that can harm millions upon millions of lives. The reason I want to be a researcher is to help people."

"That's all well and good, but you don't challenge someone as well-known and influential in the scientific world as Professor Lutz. That will kill your chances of ever becoming a credible researcher. Really, Ava, drop it! I don't want to be any part of a problem. I have a degree to finish. Please, just drop it. And like I said, we can't prove anything."

"You're right, Mike. We can't prove anything," Ava said. "Let's just go home and enjoy our weekend."

"That's a good girl." Mike gave her a condescending pat on the arm and left with a "have a great weekend."

Ava sat back down at her computer. Seeing how adamant Mike had been about keeping quiet, she'd decided not to tell him that she'd secretly sent a copy of the original data spreadsheet to her private Yahoo! email account because she'd been so happy about it. She'd wanted to study it further to make sure she'd read it correctly. Now she knew she'd spend the weekend going over the data trying to figure out how Professor Lutz had come up with his new take on the research.

She waited until all her fellow lab techs had left, then she sent a copy of the changed data to her Yahoo! account. She could compare the two against each other and try to figure out where the changes had been made. Because she would bet her life that changes *had* been made.

AS PREDICTED, AVA'S WEEKEND WAS CONSUMED WITH PORING over the first database she'd received from Professor Lutz. She went over the research from every angle she knew, but no matter how many times she went over the material and no matter how much she allowed for variables, the data showed the same results. Obesity, of and by itself, was associated with absolutely no health problems.

Just to make sure she wouldn't lose the original research, she saved the first spreadsheet on her computer hard drive and then re-emailed the data to her Yahoo! account. That way if her computer crashed or she misplaced the copy she'd made, she would still have a copy of the original data to refer to and could access it from any computer.

Then she downloaded the second set of data from her Yahoo! account and saved it on her hard drive and a USB flash drive. She didn't have time to dig into the guts of both data reports to see where the changes had been made. She'd save that until later.

After taking the USB drive containing the saved data from her computer, she was about to place it in her fireproof safety box when a strange urgency came over her to put it in a place where no one could find it. "Okay, you're getting paranoid," she told herself. But she followed the urge and put the USB drive in her purse. She was meeting her best friend, Lynn, tonight, so she'd ask Lynn to keep it for her. She'd have to confide in Lynn about the data, but Lynn would guard the secret with her own life.

SHE WATCHED LYNN WALK INTO THE RESTAURANT WHERE they'd agreed to meet and have dinner. It was uncanny how much the two of them looked alike. People not only thought they were sisters, a lot of folks insisted they must be twins. But until three years ago the two had never met. Both were five feet nine inches tall. Both had black hair, green eyes, and a milk and honey complexion. They were a larger, mixed version of Xena, Warrior Princess, and Wonder Woman.

But Ava's eyes were larger than Lynn's. And they weren't just green, they were an emerald green that practically glowed with her varied emotions. She'd been told that when she was angry her eyes would stop traffic.

One main difference was the two women's style. Lynn drove a Cadillac and Ava rode a Harley-Davidson. Ava just felt she was getting where she was going faster on a "hog." While Lynn, a Realtor, dressed like a fashion model to go to work each day, Ava was content in denim jeans, pullover T-shirts and boots. "I can't ride a bike dressed like I'm going to church," she'd tell her friend when Lynn would occasionally try to give her a makeover.

"I'm gonna kill Kibbles," Lynn started as soon as she slid into the booth. "All he's done today is look for things to chew on. Oh! And he peed on the floor once." Kibbles was her new male toy poodle. He was three months old and still in the puppy stage. Bits was the other toy poodle that she'd had for two years. He was so small when she got him that she had named him "Little Bits," but soon shortened it to Bits. So in Lynn's mind it stood to reason that she should name her second dog

Kibbles.

Ava and Lynn might look alike, but Lynn was much more ditzy than Ava. Maybe that's why Ava loved her so much. Lynn kept Ava's feet from being too attached to the ground.

"Um-hmm, and who warned you that two dogs would be a real hassle? Bits keeps you busy enough, but you just had to have another one," Ava said in an "I told you so" voice.

"You're just too serious-minded," Lynn countered. "You need to lighten up some. Be more fun-loving. How many times do I have to tell you this? You keep your head buried in all those numbers and it sucks the fun right out of you!"

"Speaking of numbers," Ava said, taking the flash drive from her purse.

"Here we go again!" Lynn moaned. But she listened with rapt attention as Ava explained what had happened.

"What are you going to do?" she asked Ava, sticking the flash drive into her purse and promising to put them in her safety firebox at home.

"I'm not sure," Ava answered, "but I know I can't just stand by and watch something like this take place."

"This makes me very nervous for you, honey," Lynn said, reaching over and taking Ava's hands in hers. "What if this leads to real trouble for you?"

"I know. I've worked really hard to get where I am. But you know that honesty has always been my policy. So if I lose my job over it, then it just has to be."

"I'm not talking about your job," Lynn said with a worried frown. "I'm talking about your life."

"My life?" Ava asked incredulously. "Why on earth would my life be in danger? We're just talking about some research data."

"Research being done by a huge drug company that stands to gain an enormous amount of money selling diet drugs based on this information. A huge drug company with enough money to make you quietly disappear."

"Whoa! Now who's being the serious one?"

"Ava, I don't feel good about this. Why don't you just let it drop? Don't try to take on the big guns at Cloneall Drugs, Inc. Quit your job if you have to. You can continue your training somewhere else."

"But Lynn, can you imagine the damage that will be done to people, especially women, if I don't say something? I've heard the diet drug Cloneall is working on could do worse harm than phen-fen, the drug combination that was so popular in the 1990s. You know how many women got sick, and some even died from valvular heart disease because of that 'miracle drug' that was supposed to help people lose weight? I can't just sit by and let that happen again! Not when I know what's going on. And I'm convinced that's why the data has been tampered with. The numbers didn't give them the answers they wanted, so they changed the numbers! Lynn, this is criminal! Would I stand by with my hands over my ears and eyes if I saw someone being murdered? This is the same thing, potentially multiplied by millions! I could never live with myself if I didn't try to stop this."

"I'm afraid, Ava. This makes me very afraid for you. Look, you don't know anything for sure, yet. Just get out before you can prove anything. Please, Ava! Get out and get far away. We can relocate. I'll give up my job and go with you, if that's what it will take to keep you safe."

"You're really serious, aren't you? I've never seen you so upset about anything, Lynn. Look, okay, I'll wait and see what happens before I start any whistleblowing. Does that make you feel better?"

"Promise?"

"Yes, I promise. Now, let's go home and get ready to start our Monday."

THREE WEEKS HAD PASSED SINCE AVA HAD GIVEN LYNN THE copied data. They had seen each other several times and talked on the phone many times, with Lynn begging Ava to walk away from the situation. Each time Ava tried to convince Lynn that she would be okay.

But today Ava was beginning to have doubts. Since Professor Lutz had returned to the lab, Mike had acted differently. He warned Ava several times to keep quiet about the changed data, and even though Ava assured him she wouldn't say anything, he was beginning to act strange around her. And today she walked in on Mike and Professor Lutz huddled over her lab computer, talking in hushed voices. When she walked into the room they started making lame excuses about checking to see if she could get online because Mike's computer seemed to be on the blink. She'd checked Mike's computer when he went to lunch and got on the Internet without any problem.

And either she *was* getting paranoid, or Professor Lutz was watching her more closely than usual.

She was barely aware of the warm sun beating down on her tense shoulders as she weaved her bike through the heavy L.A. traffic. Someone honked at her when she cut too closely between cars. Normally she would have flipped them off, but she was too preoccupied today. She headed down the small, palm-lined street where she lived. She did pay attention now. She never drove down this street without being thankful to live in such a beautiful place. She slipped the helmet off her head and draped it over the handlebars. Surely she could go one block without the helmet and not get a ticket. She loved feeling the wind in her short curly hair, and missed the days when she could ride her bike without a helmet.

The air was crisp, with very little humidity. She was tempted to head for the beach and spend the day swimming and rolling around in the sand.

Instead she parked her bike in the driveway of her small

rented house and headed up the steps to the door. Stopping to pick up a piece of gum wrapper that had blown into her flowerbed, she noticed a footprint in the mulch under her bedroom window. A big footprint. Not one of hers, for sure. A small chill made its way up her spine. *Probably just some kids,* she tried to reason with herself. *A kid with a huge foot,* her practical self answered.

As she put the key into the lock the door slid open a few inches. Frozen in her tracks, she wondered if she'd locked it this morning when she left. She *never* forgot to lock her door. In the five years of living in this house, she had never, once, forgotten to lock the door.

She should call the police before going in, she told herself, but pushed the door wide open out of curiosity. The living room was in shambles. Forgetting to be cautious, she stepped into the house and looked around. Cushions from her couch and chair lay ripped to shreds and scattered on the floor. Every drawer of her desk had been ransacked and papers covered the floor. Finally her eyes rested on the empty spot on the desk where her computer had been. Someone had trashed her home and stolen her computer.

She was about to back quietly out of the house and call the police when she saw the foot and leg protruding from the doorway that led to the kitchen and recognized Lynn's spike-heeled red shoe.

Screaming, she ran to her friend. Lynn lay in a crumpled heap with blood soaking into her hair. A huge purple lump on her head oozed blood down the side of her face.

"Oh, Lynn, please be alive. Please hang on!" Ava pleaded as she dialed 911 on her cell phone.

CHAPTER 2

VA GLANCED AROUND THE POLICE DEPARTMENT UNEASILY.
Supposedly she was waiting for the detective who had been
appointed to her case. She'd already been questioned by two
police officers and now had to go over all of it again with a detective. Why? Did they think she hit her friend over the head
and tumbled her own house?

As she waited, she relived the horror of finding Lynn in a
bleeding lump on her kitchen floor. The paramedics had ar-
rived in time to stop the bleeding and Lynn was going to be
okay. Well, if she got the hell out of Dodge, she'd be okay—
maybe.

It was obvious to Ava that someone had mistaken Lynn for
her. Someone had tried to kill her—Ava.

They had turned her house upside down looking for something. And Ava knew exactly what that "something" was. It was
made to look like a robbery, but Ava knew that whoever had
done this did it specifically to take her computer without causing a lot of suspicion as to why.

And now they would know that she had saved the original data, along with the set that had been tampered with. She
should have deleted it from her computer after saving it to the

USB drive, but she'd never dreamed that anyone would go this far.

Mike must have alerted Professor Lutz of her concern, in an effort to save his own neck.

Had Lynn been right? Were these people so determined to create a drug based on bogus data that they would kill to protect it? She was beginning to think so.

One thing was for sure. She'd make Lynn get away from this area for a while. They'd tried to kill her once, thinking she was Ava, so they'd do it again.

So where does that leave me? she wondered.

"Sorry to keep you waitin'." A voice beside her shoulder startled Ava from her troubled thoughts, causing her to violently jump.

"I'm Ricky Don McKinzie," he said, sliding into the chair behind the desk she sat beside. "I've been appointed to your case, so I'll need to go over a few things with you." The man settling himself behind the desk was easy to look at, for sure. In fact, she could spend some time looking at him. If he just hadn't talked—

"You're kidding, right?" In spite of her troubled state of mind she could barely keep from laughing out loud at the thought of this person in front of her being a detective. She suddenly felt as if she'd been dropped headfirst into a bad Matthew Mc-Conaughey movie.

"'Bout what?" he asked, finally lifting eyes the color of crystal blue glass to look at her.

That did it. A peal of laughter bubbled from her throat, grabbing the attention of several people at desks close by.

"Hi, Ricky Don," a tiny blonde said as she breezed by, causing Ava's laughter to increase a decibel.

"Are you gettin' hysterical on me? Do I need to get you some water or somethin'?"

"No! Just be quiet and give me a moment to get my breath,"

Ava managed to squeak between outbursts of laughter. The more he talked, the more she lost control.

She was calming down some when a tall brunette strolled by, flashed the man across from her a huge smile and said sweetly, "Hi, Ricky Don." And Ava was lost in a renewed attack of laughing.

Ricky Don McKinzie rose from his chair and made his way across the room. He stopped at a desk and said something to a woman who smiled sweetly and followed him back to Ava. "Ma'am, come with me, please."

After settling Ava down in a small room with a glass wall that Ava was pretty sure was a two-way mirror, the woman handed her a glass of water. "I'm Officer Judy Caldwell. I know you've been under a lot of stress after seeing your best friend almost get killed, but we don't want you going into hysterics on us."

"Then keep that country bumpkin away from me," Ava said, not too kindly.

"Excuse me?"

"You know, the guy in there. Ricky Dick, or whatever his name is. What is he doing on the L.A. police force? Or is this some kind of joke? Who talks like that? He sounds like he's straight from some *Gone With The Wind* movie, or something. But I'll have to admit he's really not that bad to look at."

"Well, around here we like to refer to him as being pure 'Deep South machismo.'"

"Machismo?"

"Yes. You know, an *exhilarating* sense of power and strength."

"Okay. Whatever turns you on. But he still sounds like a country bumpkin to me."

"That 'country bumpkin' that you keep referring to is a highly decorated, highly capable part of the LAPD. Yes, he has maintained his Mississippi drawl, but we find it rather entertaining and endearing here. And it certainly doesn't affect the way he does his job." Judy Caldwell paused for a moment, then continued. "So—is that why you were near hysterics? Because of the way he talks?"

Feeling a little sheepish, Ava said, "Well, that and his name."

"I think maybe you needed a way to relieve your tension and this is the route it found to come out."

"Maybe so. But I can't guarantee you that I won't start up again if Ricky Dick starts talking to me."

"Well, let's just test that theory." The voice had a certain sexy scratchiness to it, Ava realized as she watched him come through the door.

Looking quickly at Officer Caldwell, Ava's eyes held a question. "Yes. He's been listening to everything we said," she assured Ava.

"Oh, crap!" At least Ava still had the ability to blush when she'd embarrassed herself.

"First, let's get somethin' straight," he said, sliding into a chair close beside Ava and pinning her with the bluest gaze she'd ever seen. She became aware of quiet cologne that in a more normal setting would have reminded her of sexy maleness. "The name is Ricky Don. I'm very proud of my name. I was named after both my grandfathers, so from now on, I'd appreciate it if you'd drop the Ricky Dick thingie." His tone was slightly mocking as he drawled "thingie."

As he talked Ava felt herself being lulled into a quieter state. Was this why some Southerners were so laid back? They put each other to sleep with their talk? But she also felt just the slightest quivering of laughter trying to bubble back out.

Stop it! she silently admonished herself.

"Okay, start from the beginnin' and tell me everything that's happened."

Willing herself to control the laughter that kept trying to surface, Ava said, "I've already done that twice. Doesn't anyone take notes around here?"

"Miss Manning, if you want to live, I highly suggest you cooperate with Detective McKinzie," Officer Caldwell cut in.

"What do you mean?" Suddenly all thoughts of laughter left Ava.

"The officers who were checking for fingerprints in your house found a homemade bomb in your oven. It was rigged to go off at 4:00 this afternoon. The whole thing was supposed to look like your stove blew up and killed you. Whoever did this meant business," she said. "They also must have known about what time you'd be home. Evidence seems to indicate they wanted to tumble your place and make it look like a burglary, then have your place explode after you got home. What doesn't make sense is if they were going to blow the house up, why did they need to make it look like a burglary?"

"My guess is they figured if the stove didn't finish you off and police came on the scene, it would still look like a burglary gone bad. Do you have any idea who may have done this?" Detective McKinzie asked.

Up until now Ava had gone along with the robbery theory the police had come up with, but this was too serious to let it pass as an attempted robbery. This was attempted murder. And they had almost killed Lynn. But she still wasn't convinced that Cloneall Drugs would put a hit on her.

"I don't know who did it, but I do know they took my computer," she answered vaguely. "And I know that whoever it was doesn't know me."

"Why do you say that? They tried to kill you. You said yourself that your friend looked like you."

"Oh! Someone *was* taking notes!" Ava said.

"Why do you say they don't know you?" Detective McKinzie persisted, ignoring her sarcasm.

"Because they tried to kill Lynn. See, anyone who knows me knows that I don't wear red spiked heels and flimsy dresses like Lynn had on. I wear exactly what you see. Jeans, T-shirt, boots."

"Maybe they thought you'd dressed up to go out for some reason," Officer Caldwell said.

"Those who know me also know that I don't dress up even to go out. I just don't care about all the froufrou stuff."

"So what did they think you had on your computer that was important enough to kill you—or Lynn—for?" Detective McKinzie asked. "Apparently Lynn came into your home earlier than they were expecting you, so they had to silence her, thinking it was you. They knew the bomb would take care of her when it went off."

"Personally, I think it was a mistaken address," Ava hedged, then silently patted herself on the back for coming up with that so quickly. If she could convince them someone had the wrong house, it would give her a little more time to do some sleuthing on her own.

"The wrong address?" Two voices echoed.

"Sure. It looks to me like whoever tried to pull this off just got confused as to which house they were supposed to hit. It happens all the time. Even the police raid the wrong house sometimes."

"She's got a point," Officer Caldwell said. "Remember the Jones case?

"Yeah," Detective McKinzie said, as a pained look crossed his face. Ava imagined he had been in on that one.

"So what you're sayin' is that these people mistakenly broke into your house, stole your computer, thinkin' it was someone else's, and left your friend for dead, knowin' that the house was goin' to go up in an explosion?" Skepticism was apparent in his every word.

"That's what it looks like to me," Ava said and shrugged her shoulders, hoping she was convincing.

"Okay. Look. Just to be safe, don't go home tonight. Do you have somewhere to stay?" Officer Caldwell asked.

"I plan to stay at the hospital with Lynn. They're keeping her overnight for observation. Then I'll go home with her for a few days until I know she's okay." *And try to convince her to leave town*, she thought.

"Promise to let us know if you hear or see anything?" Officer Caldwell asked, standing. Apparently the questioning was over, Ava thought with relief.

"Yes, I promise. Thank you for your help," Ava said, offering her hand to Officer Caldwell.

"And, thank you, Detective Ricky Dick," she smiled sweetly as she breezed past him and left the room.

"Is she the only female who has ever challenged you?" Judy asked. She watched the emotions swirl across Ricky Don McKinzie's face as he swiped his hand through his light brown, slightly curly hair.

"It might be easy to understand why someone would try to kill her," he smirked. "Personally, I don't buy the mistaken house story she's tryin' to feed us." He stormed back to his desk.

Officer Judy Caldwell grinned. She'd seen Ricky Don McKinzie go through every woman's heart on the force, hers included. She'd kind of like to see him brought to his knees. Even if it was another woman who did it.

AT THE HOSPITAL, AVA TOLD LYNN ABOUT HER ENCOUNTER with the country-talking detective. She had Lynn laughing so hard that a nurse came in to check the monitor so see if she was okay.

"Now, she needs to be taking it easy," the nurse admonished Ava. "She's had a very hard bump on her head."

"Okay," Ava said, feeling like a chastised schoolgirl. But as soon as the nurse left the room, the two friends started laughing again.

But soon, Ava got serious. "Lynn, you have to go stay with

your parents for a while. You've been talking about how much you missed home. Can you get a leave of absence from work? I mean, surely if you tell them you had an attempt on your life, they'll let you take a few weeks off. Just until I can get to the bottom of this."

"What do you mean so you can get to the bottom of this? Aren't the police going to help you find out who did this?"

"I told them I think the people who attacked you had mistaken the address. I want to see if I can figure it out before I make a big deal of it."

"Sweetie, my head feels like a big deal has already been made out of it," Lynn stated emphatically.

"But it really could have been a mistaken address and you just walked in on them. Right?"

"The guy who hit me called me by your name."

"What?"

"He said, 'Sleep tight, Ava,' and the next thing I knew I felt like my skull was shattering into a million tiny pieces."

"You didn't mention that to anyone?"

"No. I thought you'd want to know it first."

"Oh, Lynn. I'm so sorry. You have to get out of this town for a while."

"But I don't want to leave you. Come with me. We can both disappear for a while. I warned you from the beginning that this could turn dangerous, but you wouldn't listen to me! Promise me that you'll leave town with me."

"You know I can't. You know I have to follow this through. I just can't quit now."

"You're the most stubborn woman—no, you're the most stubborn *person* I've ever known. And it may get you killed! Is it worth it?"

"Yes. Now get some rest. You've had quite a bump on your head!" Ava mimicked the nurse.

THREE DAYS LATER FOUND AVA ON HER WAY BACK TO THE LAB at Cloneall Drugs. She'd managed to get Lynn to rest for those days, but hadn't yet convinced her that she needed to leave town for a while. Lynn kept saying that she'd go if Ava would go with her.

Ava tried to act as natural and normal as she did every day when she walked into the lab. But her attempts to be normal went unheeded, as nobody was in the lab yet.

She sat down at her computer and turned it on, but couldn't access it. It told her that her password had been denied. She tried several times, but each time was denied.

Her temperature was quickly rising when she heard the door open. She glanced up to see Mike walking in.

"Good morning, Mike," she greeted, like she always did.

"*Ava?*" Mike was obviously shaken to see her at her computer. "I—we—I thought you were—"

"Dead?" Ava filled in for him. She'd planned to act like business as usual, but her anger at finding her password deleted from the system, and seeing his reaction, totally eradicated any nonchalance she may have planned.

"No! Well—we did hear that you'd had an incident at your home."

"So you assumed I was dead? I mean, someone must have assumed that, because my password has been deleted from the system. So it looks like nobody was expecting me to come back."

"What? Your password doesn't work?"

"Nope. It says I'm denied access. Do you know anything about this?"

"No! Professor Lutz said—I mean—"

"I'll take it from here, Mike." Professor Lutz spoke from the back of the room. Had he been there all the time? She hadn't seen anyone when she came in.

"Ava, it was brought to our attention that you weren't too

happy with the data from our research, so we've decided to let you go from your position."

"And break into my house and steal my computer and try to kill me? Did you decide to do that too, Professor Lutz?"

"I'm quite sure I don't know what you're talking about, Ava. Now you need to leave, or I'll have security escort you off the premises."

"Can I ask one question?"

"I suppose," he answered.

"Who brought my unhappiness to your attention?" Ava looked directly at Mike when she asked the question.

"You were overheard discussing it," Professor Lutz said. "Now you need to leave. And Ava, I wouldn't suggest you discuss your opinion of what went on in this lab to anyone. It's a dangerous world out there. Big companies like Cloneall Drugs don't like whistleblowers."

"And I'm sure high-and-mighty research scientists don't like them, either." Ava saw Professor Lutz reaching for the security button on his phone and said, "Don't bother, Professor Klutz, I'm going." She saw fury sweep over his face at her deliberate misuse of his name.

"Ava!" Mike called to her.

"Let her go, Mike. You've done all you can."

AVA BRIEFLY WORRIED ABOUT MIKE AS SHE POINTED HER bike toward home. Had Mike told Professor Lutz her concern over the data? But she hadn't told Mike that she'd copied the first set of data, so Professor Lutz had to assume she might have copied it and had her computer stolen. What was Mike about to tell her that Professor Lutz had said?

She had no doubt that Professor Lutz had been threatening her. And that left no doubt about what had happened at her house and to Lynn. These people were serious about their falsified data.

She knew she'd have to tell LAPD about her conversation sooner or later, but right now she wanted to go home and see how much damage was done. Detective Ricky Dick might not want her going to her house, but that was his problem, not hers.

She called Lynn and told her that she wasn't at work, but was going to make a few stops before going back to Lynn's.

She drove her bike in from a side street that wasn't traveled much, and parked in the back of her house, just in case someone was watching.

Yellow crime scene ribbon circled her entire home, but wasn't that hard to step over. The first thing she saw when she entered the back door was a circle of dried blood in the kitchen floor. Lynn's blood. It should have been her blood. Her heart pounded as she walked quickly past it, trying not to remember Lynn lying there so hurt and helpless She hurried into the living room.

The curtains were drawn, keeping out all the light, and Ava knew better than to try and turn on a lamp. Anyone could be watching her house.

Everything looked basically like it had the day she'd last seen it. Her things were scattered all over the floor. Couch cushions, throw pillows, knick-knacks—some broken—magazines, papers and unpaid bills lay strewn everywhere. Some of her papers had been thrown into the fireplace that centered the room. Suddenly her life felt like the floor looked.

"It can all be fixed," a voice said from a dark corner.

"Crap! What are you doing here?" Already she'd recognize that lazy, scratchy voice anywhere.

"Lynn said you'd probably head this way," he answered, coming closer to her.

"You talked with Lynn? Why? When? Why?"

"In case you forgot, Lynn was hit over the head a few days ago, and needs to make a statement to the LAPD. I kind of

25

have to talk with her to get a statement." Amusement sent his eyes into blue twinkling fireworks that Ava could see even in the dimly lit room.

"Plus she's worried about you. Despite your casual manner about this case, she's convinced that you're in danger." By now he was standing close enough for her to be aware of his cologne.

Why did his cologne send her imagination into double-time? She'd never even paid that much attention to a man's cologne. Yet now, surrounded by the clutter of her former life and not knowing what lay ahead of her, this country bumpkin whom she had laughed at a few days ago was causing other emotions to stir.

She had to get out of here. Had to get back to Lynn's. The doom and gloom of this room was making her lose her mind.

"I've got to go," she said, turning for the door.

"You goin' back to Lynn's?" he asked.

"Yes, I'm goin' back to Lynn's," she mimicked.

"You're a quick learner," he grinned as he pulled the back door closed and locked it behind them. "It won't be long before you'll be talkin' just like a Southerner."

For the first time Ava felt the full impact of his beautiful smile directed at her. And now she almost understood why those women in the LAPD were practically swooning over him.

And that made her angry. "Bite me!" she muttered, and swung her leg over her bike.

"My pleasure," he promised, and laughed as she roared from the driveway.

If he weren't so worried about her, he would really enjoy this case.

CHAPTER 3

From habit, Ava woke up at 7 a.m. sharp the next morning. Her first urge was to get up and get dressed for work, then she remembered that she wouldn't be going back to the lab.

Brief sadness washed over her at the loss of what she had considered a wonderful opportunity. But the sadness was quickly followed by hot anger and a determination to get to the bottom of the façade of Cloneall Drugs and Professor Kiss-Ass Lutz.

She might be a little nobody in their opinion and by their standards, but purpose and tenacity could go a long way in getting what a person wanted. And she wanted *them*. Bad.

She'd come too far in her pursuit of a dream career to just lie down and roll over when things went bad. If she was going to lose that dream, she might as well take a few people down with her.

What kind of game was Mike playing? She could understand Professor Lutz. Maybe. No. She couldn't understand how someone as talented as he was could take a chance on losing everything he'd worked so hard for. And Mike was so close to actually holding his dream in his hands. Did he think Professor

Lutz could put him on the fast track to realize that dream?

Her cell phone playing the theme song to *Dr. Zhivago* snapped her out of her thoughts. Glancing at the caller I.D., she saw the LAPD number and assumed it would be the irritating Detective McKinzie.

"You're in a hurry to get started this morning," she snapped into the phone.

"Did you know a Mike Campbell who worked at Cloneall Drugs?"

"Oh, crap! What's happened to him?" Fear, cold and sharp, invaded Ava's brain.

"He was found on the beach this morning. Apparently he drowned."

"I seriously doubt that," Ava said. "He was an avid surfer in his free time. In fact, according to him his meager apartment barely put him in a bracket above 'beach bum.'"

"So you suspect foul play?"

"I highly suspect foul play," she answered forcefully.

"Why do you think that?"

"I just do," she hedged. She wasn't ready to tell him about her conversation with Professor Lutz and Mike—but for Mike's sake she knew she should. Although it wouldn't do him any good now.

"Okay, I'm hearin' a lot of things you're not sayin'," Detective McKinzie said. "Can you come down to the morgue and identify him? We haven't been able to locate any family. Do you know anything about his family?"

"He said he didn't have a family. He lived with his grandmother until he got old enough to go out on his own. But that's all I know. He was intrigued with research, and I think that's why he didn't want to stand up to Professor Lutz about some data that was changed."

"I don't believe you've mentioned anything about that to me."

"Well, there are a couple of things I haven't mentioned. I guess after I identify him, you and I need to have a talk."

"It would seem so. How soon can you be here?"

"In an hour," she said, and hung up the phone.

MIKE HAD BEEN MURDERED. SHE WAS CONVINCED OF IT. AND the anger pit in her stomach deepened.

Standing in the cold morgue, looking down at Mike's slightly blue, very swollen face, a shudder ran through Ava's body. She welcomed Detective McKinzie's arm, which automatically came around her shoulders at her involuntary shudder.

"Is it him?" he asked.

"Yes," was all she could choke out, as she turned and hurried from the room that was as ice-cold as death itself.

AVA ALLOWED DETECTIVE MCKINZIE TO HOLD HER ARM AND guide her to a private room, where he pulled out a chair for her to sit, then handed her a box of tissue. He sat down across from her and waited until she had regained her composure.

"Were you close?" he asked after a few minutes.

"Not really. But he seemed like a good guy. I'm upset that he lost his life, but I'm more upset because I'm the reason he did."

"Don't take the blame for something you're not sure of," he cautioned.

"Oh, I'm very sure of it," Ava answered, looking at him through tears that turned her green eyes into jade pools of sadness, mystery, and a little fear.

"When you think you're ready, I know a quaint little coffee shop where we can talk without being noticed."

"I'm ready," she answered, and stood.

"You want to ride with me?" Detective McKinzie asked as they made their way outside.

"No, I'll ride my bike."

"Do you know where Just Like Grandma's is?"

"Yes! Lynn and I love to go there."

"Okay. I'll meet you there. Just wait until I drive around here. I'll be in a red Mustang."

A red Mustang. Of course. What else would a country-talking, charming-as-hell detective on the LAPD force drive?

She'd barely fastened her helmet into place before she heard the loud pipes of a car approaching. Ava knew cars. If she ever owned a car, it would be just like the one she watched slowly approach. A Rangoon red 1964 1/2 Mustang convertible with a black top and interior. The wheels sported special rims and hubs.

"Now that's a car!" Ava said as he stopped beside her.

"You like it?"

"I want it!" For the first time she dropped her defenses with him, and looked at his car in open admiration. "What's under the hood?"

Pleased that she would ask such a question, Ricky Don got out of the car and raised the hood. "It has a 289 cubic inch V8 carburetor with a straight transmission," he said, watching the look of awe on her face. He was happy his car had taken her mind off of Mike for a moment.

And at that moment, he was halfway in love. He'd never known a woman he could express his love of cars to without having her eyes glaze over and seeing her mind close down.

"Would you like to drive it sometime?"

"You'd let me drive this?" she asked, looking up. She hadn't realized how close they were standing, huddled under the hood of the car. Again she was impacted by his face. His smile. But mostly by his eyes, which could change with each emotion crossing his mind. Right now she couldn't read the emotion she saw. One she'd never seen in his eyes before. And that sent up little warning signals.

"I guess we'd better get on with our talk," she said quickly, and got back on her bike.

Hmm. Wonder what scared her off this time, Ricky Don thought as he slowly led them to the street and headed toward Just Like Grandma's.

After being seated in a back booth by an older woman who gushed over Ricky Don, they ordered coffee.

"Have you had breakfast?" he asked.

"No, just a swig of coffee before I dashed from Lynn's apartment."

"They have wonderful cinnamon rolls. Why don't we let Martha bring us a couple." Before she could answer he asked Martha to add two cinnamon rolls. "This way, she'll leave us alone for awhile and not keep tryin' to feed us," he explained.

He'd arranged their seating so Ava faced the wall and he faced the incoming traffic. The place was a tiny, quaint nook on a side street, but she could hear the door constantly opening and closing. Apparently they did a big business from people dashing in to get food to go.

"Hmm. This is delicious!" Ava said after a couple of bites of the warm cinnamon roll.

"They're the best I've ever had. My Gramma couldn't even make 'em like this," he said. "They have a lady in the back who makes 'em from scratch every mornin'. She won't give anyone her recipe. People constantly ask her for it."

Ava knew he was making small talk, so she put her fork down and began. She started from the moment she'd seen the first data set and told him everything. As she got into her story, she relaxed and realized how easy he was to talk to. His eyes never wavered from hers. His attention was on every word she said, and she had no doubt he could repeat them to her almost word for word.

"Okay," he said when she'd finished. "I believe you're in real danger. But why? Why would a company as large as Cloneall Drugs try to tamper with data? If the data said obesity wasn't a health threat, why not go with that? I expect a lot of folks would love to hear that!"

"But that doesn't sell diet drugs. They're working on a new drug that they'll try to sell to everyone they can. But first they have to convince as many people as possible that they're fat and unhealthy and need the drug. They have to make people believe their very lives are in danger if they carry *any* extra weight.

"They're already working on that as hard as they can, but this is a huge study, and if they can use this research to convince people that any 'excess' weight is a real threat, the sales of their new diet drug will make them billions upon billions of dollars."

"Have you ever dieted?" he asked, looking closely at Ava.

"Most of my childhood and teens," she answered.

"Why?"

"My parents thought I was too fat. I think I was an embarrassment to them. I was an only child and they wanted me to be perfect."

"Do you diet now?"

"Nope. I decided that I was born to look like I do, so I won't ever be forced to go on another diet."

"Good! I'd hate to see you lose any of those curves!" His playful wink caused an unexpected jolt through Ava's body.

"Look, Ricky Dick, if we're going to have to work closely on this case, don't get any ideas about us being closer than a working relationship. I don't just jump into bed with every guy who comes along."

"Good. Because I'd sure be pissed if I thought you did. And it's Ricky Don, please."

Before Ava could reply, he stood and went to the cash register to pay for their meal. She had little choice but to follow him.

Once they were outside, he turned to her. "I want you to meet me at Lynn's. We have to work on a plan to keep you and her safe."

"But I was going shopping. I need to pick up a few things."

"Not a good idea. I'll follow you to Lynn's, and after we talk about what to do next, I'll go with you shoppin', if you just have to go."

"You'll go with me?" Horrified that he was going to try to be her constant companion and bodyguard, Ava felt every fiber in her body rebelling.

"Yep. I'm goin' with you. Now, if you don't mind, let's take this discussion to Lynn's. I don't feel real safe out here on the street like this, after what you've just told me."

"Lynn, it seems we're on our way to your apartment," Ava informed her friend from her cell phone headset as she maneuvered her bike into the oncoming traffic.

"I know. Detective McKinzie just called to ask if this is a good time. I'm so glad you told him, Ava."

"Oh, so he *informs* me we're doing something, but he *asks* you? Amazing."

"Well, Ava, you know you're just trying to get under his skin with that Ricky Dick thing. You should be ashamed of that. He's just trying to help you. And he's so cute!"

"Oh, no! He's already gotten to you with that quaint Southern charm, hasn't he."

"Maybe. Now I have to put on some makeup before y'all get here." Lynn hung up the phone before Ava could say anything.

"This sucks!" Ava yelled, not caring that the driver next to her sent her a questioning glare.

Detective McKinzie pulled into the parking space beside Ava as she stepped off her bike. She resented the fact that he'd stayed on her tail the entire trip. Being a cop, he knew better than to tailgate her like that. If she'd skidded her bike, he'd have run right over it and her.

"Think you could have driven any closer to me? What if I'd

wrecked my bike? You'd have killed me." Anger shot green daggers from her eyes.

Grabbing her arm and heading toward Lynn's apartment, he glanced around before practically dragging her to the door.

Before he could knock, Lynn swung the door open. She was about to speak when the two almost ran over her before Detective McKinzie slammed the door and locked it.

"What the hell is wrong with you?" Ava ground out.

"The reason I was so close behind you was to keep Mr. Bigg from cutting me off and getting behind you."

"What are you talking about?" Ava asked. She'd been so caught up in her thoughts she hadn't noticed anything except him riding her tail.

"A huge man in a black van kept tryin' to shove me over so he could get behind you. I knew it wasn't a matter of him just passin', because there was plenty of room in the other lane. Or he could have dropped back behind me. But he wanted behind you, real bad. I don't think he had good intentions toward you either. He kept shootin' me the bird because I wouldn't move over for him. I finally flashed my badge at him, so he fell in behind me but kept followin' us."

"So he knows we came into this apartment complex?" Ava asked. Now they would know where Lynn lived.

"Yep. I'm positive he saw us make the turn. I don't know if he turned in or not, but he knows we did."

"Lynn, you can't stay here. You have to go to your parents' for a while. I'm so sorry I've brought this on you, but they killed Mike and I'd sooner die myself than have them murder you. Please go." She wrapped her friend in her arms and held her tightly.

"I think she's right, Lynn," Detective McKinzie agreed. "These people seem to mean business."

"I told her I'd go if she did," Lynn said. She patted the bandage on her head. "The doctor said this could come off tomorrow. I can be packed and carry my luggage to the doctor's office with me. Ricky Don, maybe you could carry us to the airport."

"Lynn, I'm not running from a bunch of bullies. I have to stay here. Please understand. But this is my fight, not yours. And I can't allow you to get hurt anymore in the mix."

"Ricky Don, make her come with me. You can catch the bad guys without her. In fact, she'll probably just get in your way. She's so pushy, she'll be telling you how to do your job. She can really get on your nerves, if you let her."

"Lynn! You're supposed to be my friend! How can you say those things?"

"Well, I love you, but the truth's still the truth."

Ricky Don watched the exchange between the two women. They were so much alike, yet so different. Ava had on faded jeans and a T-shirt. Lynn had on a pair of slacks, a frilly blouse and heels, even though she was walking around with a bandage on her head and should have been resting in bed.

Suddenly he had an idea.

"Lynn, do you mind if I look in your closet?" Before she could answer he headed to her bedroom.

"Is he always this presumptuous?" Lynn asked Ava.

"Only about 100 percent of the time that I've been around him," Ava said.

"I think I have the answer," he said, coming back into the room. "Lynn, you go to your parents' for a few weeks, but leave most of your clothes here. Ava, you can become Lynn. You look like you wear the same size clothes."

"That's a wonderful idea!" Lynn squealed. "You can even drive my Cadillac. Nobody will recognize you if you're out of those jeans and off that bike!"

"I think you're both forgetting that *you* were the one who got hit over the head. *You're* the one they called by my name when they hit you. And you were dressed like Lynn, not me."

"Oh, yeah. I forgot."

35

"They called you by her name when they hit you?" Detective McKinzie's questioning glance darted from one to the other. "And when were you goin' to tell me this little bit of information?" This time his eyes drilled into Ava's.

"I forgot?"

"What else have you forgotten? Ava, I can't do my job if you keep information from me."

It was the first time he'd called her by name, and Ava didn't like the butterflies that took flight in her insides. "I was going to tell you today. I really did forget."

"Is there anything else?"

"Not that I can think of, but I promise if I think of something I'll tell you. I want to catch these thugs. I really want to catch them for what they did to Lynn and Mike, and what they want to do to millions of other innocent people."

"If they called Lynn by your name, do you think they know you? Or do you know them?"

"No. I think Professor Lutz, or someone, hired them to kill me. I think they had a name and an address, but I don't think they'd ever seen me before. And I can assure you nobody in this city has ever seen me in anything except jeans and a T-shirt. Lynn can back me up on that. She's constantly bitching at me to dress up a little. She really wants me to be a diva."

"Well, I may be able to dress you up some day, but a diva? I don't think that will ever happen," Lynn chimed in.

"Then you'll become Lynn and disguise yourself so we can have a little more freedom to move around?"

"If it'll mean that Lynn will go away for awhile and it'll help us get to the bottom of this, yes. As bad as I hate to—okay."

CHAPTER 4

L YNN WAS SAFELY ON A PLANE TO NASHVILLE, TN. HER
parents were thrilled that she was finally coming for a visit.
They didn't know why she had suddenly made the decision
to come home, but were happy that she had. She'd even had
Kibbles and Bits flown to Nashville. She said she didn't want
to leave them, since she didn't know how long she'd be gone.

Ava gazed at the small gathering around Mike's freshly dug
grave. She didn't recognize most of the people there, but knew
by the way they dressed that they were some of Mike's surfing
friends.

It's a beautiful day to be buried, Ava thought as she watched
the soft, fluffy clouds float overhead. Songbirds chirped in a
nearby tree. But the call of the seagulls in the distance haunted
her. She knew they dipped and soared over the waves Mike
loved so much, but would never ride again. And it was her
fault.

And it was her fault!

She finally let reality sink in. This young man that she barely
knew was forever closed in a sealed casket, about to be lowered
into the cold damp ground, and it was her fault.

Oh, Mike, I'm so sorry, she silently said to the waiting casket.

I'm so sorry! But I will get these guys. They'll pay for what they did to you. I promise you that!

Fiery determination replaced the grief that had filled her eyes, as she looked up into the curious glance of Professor Lutz. But his eyes only held mild disinterest as they slid away to look anywhere except Mike's coffin.

Fear lurched instantly into Ava's throat, but gradually subsided when she realized that he hadn't recognized her.

Relief flooded her. He didn't recognize her! Then she almost smiled, remembering what she had on.

Detective McKinzie had agreed that she could go to the funeral alone after she'd told him what she was wearing. He'd had a meeting this morning, and had barely made it back to the department on time after taking Lynn to the airport.

Ava wore a black dress, black hat with a veil over her face, and black heels. Lynn had bought the outfit from a second-hand store to wear to last year's Halloween party at her office. Ava's own mother wouldn't recognize her.

She wished suddenly that she could go home to her mother. To feel her mom's comforting arms around her and hear her say that "everything will be okay," like her mom always did. But that was impossible. Everything didn't work out okay for her mom when she lost control of her car two years ago on an icy highway and was killed instantly when the car smashed into a tree. She'd been on her way home from a New Year's Eve party when the accident happened. Ava missed her terribly, sometimes.

After Mike's brief service she made her way back to Lynn's older model Cadillac. The car had belonged to Lynn's grandmother, who willed it to Lynn when she died. Lynn didn't care if the car was old. It was a Cadillac and it had been her grandmother's, so she loved it and drove it with pride.

The car was immaculate and had only 52,000 miles on it. It had been kept in a garage until Lynn got it. It had a basic black exterior with a tan interior, so Ava felt comfortable that it didn't draw a lot of attention. She'd much rather be on her bike, but, for now, this had to do.

She didn't see the two men dressed in black who wrote down the license plate as she left the cemetery.

"DO YOU KNOW WHO THAT WAS?" THE FIRST MAN IN BLACK asked.

"Nope. Never saw her before," the second man answered.

"But she had to have known Mike. Why else would she have been at his funeral?"

"Maybe it was someone from the grocery store! Hell, it's not possible for us to know every single person he knew."

"Well, there's one thing for sure. We have to find out who she is and if she knows anything. She's the only one at the funeral that we don't recognize. We have the particulars on the rest of them."

AVA LET HERSELF INTO LYNN'S APARTMENT. IT SEEMED SO strange to be here, knowing that Lynn was in the air flying to another state. She stood in the living room and glanced around the apartment, seeing all of Lynn's things, and again remembered Lynn lying in a pool of blood. Yes, it was best that she left town for a while.

The living room, dining area and kitchen were one big open room. There was a hallway that led to the only bedroom, which had its own bath. There was a small half-bath off the hallway, just before the bedroom.

After wandering around the apartment for a few minutes, she came up with an idea. She needed to know for sure if her new look would actually fool anyone, so she dressed in a mint green sundress, added a white short-sleeve jacket that stopped at the waist, and slipped on white sandals.

Looking at her reflection in the mirror, she looked like

Lynn, but something was missing. After studying her face for a few moments, she said, "Oh, crap! I'm going to have to wear that war paint she wears before anyone will think I'm Lynn."

After digging through several drawers, she found makeup. Trying to remember how Lynn used the stuff, she applied foundation, blush, eyeshadow, mascara and lip gloss that tasted like strawberries. Her face felt as if it would crack if she barely smiled.

But taking a second glance in the mirror, she felt reassured. She barely recognized herself.

Not half bad, she thought, then, horrified, hurried from the apartment. She would *not* start liking this look for herself. She was a motorcycle-riding type of girl, not the girly-girl that had looked back at her.

Ava walked briskly into the shop where she and Lynn bought most of their clothes. Susan, who had worked there for years, said, "Hi, Lynn! Where's your sidekick? You two seldom ever come in here without the other."

"She had to do some chores today, and I really needed to pick up a few things," Ava answered, happy that Susan didn't recognize her.

"How can I help you?" Susan asked.

"I need some new shoes," Ava said, heading directly to the work boot section.

"You looking for something for Ava?" Susan asked.

Realizing what she'd done, Ava quickly headed to the casual shoes. She might have to dress like Lynn, but she didn't have to wear these dreadful heels all day. At least she could wear some flats.

"No, but these do remind me of her. I wonder if I'll ever get her out of those jeans, T-shirts and clunker shoes," Ava said, and picked out three pair of casual flats, all in the same style. One pair in black, one pair in tan and one pair in white. These should match anything in Lynn's closet, she reasoned.

"You don't usually go for the flats," Susan commented. "You usually go straight to the heels."

"I'm going to be standing more at work, so I thought I'd better go for the more practical shoe," Ava lied.

Breathing a deep sigh of relief that Susan hadn't recognized her, she returned to Lynn's car. Two men dressed in black leaned casually against a car parked close to her. Where had she seen them before? Something niggled at her subconscious. Were they waiting for her?

She eased out of the parking lot, watching in her rear-view mirror. They got in a black van, but didn't follow her.

Relaxing, she chided herself for becoming paranoid.

Okay, what now? She sure didn't plan to go back and sit in Lynn's apartment all day. Suddenly she longed to go home. She wanted to go clean up the mess that had been made. Wanted to reclaim the space where she'd gone to relax and unwind every day. But she knew she couldn't go there now. Maybe sometime in the late night she'd sneak over there and have a look around.

That thought gave her comfort. But she still didn't know what to do with her day.

"This is going to really get on my nerves," she spoke aloud. "I've got to do something! Maybe I'll get a job."

As if on cue, her cell phone rang.

"Where are you?" Ricky Don's drawl seemed to crawl through the phone.

"I've been shopping," she said, remembering he'd told her not to go alone.

"You what?" The drawl sharpened.

"I wanted to see if Susan would recognize me. Lynn and I go to her shop all the time, so I was testing my new look. She didn't recognize me, so I'm happy about that. She thought I was Lynn."

"You on your way home?"

"I was thinking about it, but decided I'd better not go there."

"You know what I mean, Ava. Are you on your way to Lynn's?"

"No. I don't plan to just sit around her apartment all day. I may look for a job."

"I don't think that would be a very good idea. How are you going to help me find the bad guys if you have to work all day?"

"Hmm. There's always that."

"Meet me at Lynn's," he said, and hung up.

"I don't like pushy men," Ava spoke to the phone. But she headed toward the apartment.

As Ava turned into the apartment complex she recognized the black van from Susan's shop, turning in behind her. So they had followed her! What should she do now?

Call Ricky Don, a little voice whispered.

"Oh, shut up!" She admonished her own head as she dialed his number.

"Yes?"

"I'm being followed by two men in black, driving a black van."

"Okay. Act innocent. Come on and park. I'll be waitin' for you, but don't acknowledge me unless it's necessary."

Casually, Ava got out of the Cadillac and headed toward the walkway to the apartment door. She'd spotted Ricky Don leaning against his Mustang, sipping from a "to go" cup from McDonald's.

"Excuse me, ma'am? Could I ask you a question?" The tall man in black was coming toward her.

"I don't usually talk to strangers," Ava said, and kept on walking.

He reached out and grabbed her arm to detain her. From the corner of her eye she saw Ricky Don go completely still.

"Take your hands off of me," Ava said quietly.

"I'm sorry, but I really need to ask you something. Where is your friend? The one who rides a motorcycle? We need to talk with her."

"Who are 'we'?" Ava asked.

"My partner and I. We saw you at Mike's funeral, but we didn't see her. Ava is her name, right? She and Mike were very close friends, and we need to talk with her."

So that's where she'd seen them, Ava realized. She also realized they didn't know her or Mike very well or they would have known that they weren't "very close friends."

Taking a chance that these weren't the goons who had attacked Lynn at her house, Ava said, "Haven't you heard? She was attacked at her home and is in really bad shape. They had to send her home to her family to get well."

"Oh, and where would that be?" By now the second man in black had joined them. Something about his pale blue eyes gave Ava the creeps.

"I can't tell you that, because you may be one of the people who attacked her. Now go away." Ava started to turn away when the tall one caught her arm again.

"Hey, darlin'! Who are your friends?" Ricky Don came up to Ava, wrapped a possessive arm around her shoulders, and planted a kiss on her lips. "I can't leave you alone for two minutes without some guy hittin' on you."

Smiling and extending his hand to the tall man, he continued, "Hi! I'm Ricky Don McKinzie. Can I help you boys?"

"We just wanted to ask the lady about her friend."

Aftershocks from the unexpected kiss rippled through Ava's body. And because she felt something— *anything*—because of the kiss, she was instantly angry.

"What do you want with her? You want to try and kill her again?" She stepped closer to the man who had grabbed her arm. "You tell that asshole Klutz that he'd better leave my friend alone if he knows what's good for him!"

"What the lady means," Ricky Don said, "is that you boys

need to get on out of town before you wind up like Mike did."

"What do you know about Mike?" Both men swarmed Ricky Don as if they were about to wrestle him to the ground. But Ricky Don didn't blink an eye as he calmly said, "I know he's dead."

"We'll find her without your help. She can't hide forever." They turned and headed for the black van.

Ava started toward the apartment, but Ricky Don caught her arm. "Wait, I don't want them seeing which apartment we go in," he said, still holding onto her arm even as the van pulled from the parking lot.

"You can unhand me now," Ava said, and tugged to pull her arm free.

"They might come back," Ricky Don said, gripping her arm and leading her to the apartment door, where he produced a key and unlocked the door and proceeded to lead them in.

"What are you doing with a key to this apartment?"

But instead of answering, Ricky Don pulled her to him and captured her lips in a brain-fogging kiss.

For a brief moment Ava was overcome with the sheer power of his lips on hers. She'd never had anyone kiss her like this. She almost forgot to protest. Almost—

"What are you doing?" she sputtered, shoving away from him.

"I'm doin' what I've wanted to do from the first day I met you. The meetin' with the black suits outside gave me a perfect reason to kiss you. Even that spur-of-the-moment kiss was better than I'd expected. So I had to do it again just to see if your lips were really as delicious the second time as the first."

"Delicious? You're calling a kiss delicious?" Ava headed for the sofa to sit down and try to cover up the fact that she was trembling from head to toe.

"Yep. Delicious. Your lips look delicious and I wanted to taste them. And they are delicious. In fact, I think I've got to have more." He headed toward her.

Ava jumped up from the sofa and went to the kitchen to put on a pot of coffee, but he followed her.

"Look," she said, keeping her back to him and filling the coffee pot with water and coffee. "You're a policeman—a detective on the LAPD. I'm a woman with a price on my head, it seems. There's no room in our lives for hanky-panky."

He didn't answer, so she turned around—right into his arms. "Hanky-panky?" he said, sliding his hands up and down her arms. "Hanky-panky? Is that what you call slow, easy, mindblowin' lovemakin'?"

His voice was barely above a whisper, which only intensified the gravelly timbre. Blue eyes held hers as she felt her insides turning to hot liquid. Feelings as foreign to her as his Southern drawl engulfed her, causing her to panic.

She stepped quickly to the side and around him, giving herself enough space to breath.

"Look, Ricky Dick, this just won't work," she said after gasping a few breaths of air. "We're as different as two people can be. Now go home and leave me alone."

She'd never known anyone could move as quickly as he did. Before she saw him coming he had her hands pinned behind her back and his face was lowered to hers. His lips featherbrushed hers as he said, "Every time you call me Ricky Dick, I'm goin' to kiss you breathless. Like this," he said as he gently brushed kisses on the corners of her mouth. "And like this." He captured her lips in his so lightly that she could barely feel his lips on hers. But the sensation was staggering. His tongue traced her lips twice before he raised his head and said, "I want to hear you call me by my correct name."

"Detective McKinzie," she barely whispered.

He was lowering his mouth to hers again and she said with a stronger voice, "Ricky Don. Okay, you win. Now are you happy?"

"Only just barely," he smiled, as he released her pinned hands but rested his hands on her waist, with his thumbs lightly brushing the bottom of her breasts.

"You have to go," she said, pulling away from hands that were wreaking havoc with what little control she had left.

"Not yet. We need to talk about what's happened. First, to answer your question about the key, Lynn had an extra one and she gave it to me. She said she'd feel better if I could get in the apartment in case you needed me."

Several sardonic remarks ran through Ava's mind, but she didn't speak. She knew Lynn was just trying to protect her.

"Second," he continued, "it appears that two different interests are trying to get to you. We had the big guy in the black van trying to cut me off and get behind you the other day. Now these two goons, also in a black van, but a newer model than Big Bubba's. Do you have any idea who any of these people are?"

"None. But I'm ready to find out. Look, you're the detective, don't you have any leads yet?"

"I'm sorry, but you know as much as I do. Forensics dusted your place for fingerprints, but didn't find a single one. These guys are professionals. They knew what they were doing."

He barely saw the fear flit through her eyes before she controlled it. "Incidentally, I love the way you fill out your jeans and T-shirts, but you're hotter'n hell in that dress. I'd love to slowly take it off of you and kiss you all over."

"Go home, Ricky Di—Don," she said, in a voice that she knew didn't convince anyone.

As RICKY DON MCKINZIE MADE HIS WAY TO HIS CAR, ALL HE could think was, "Daa-yam! Now *that's* a woman!"

He didn't notice the black van that fell in behind him and followed him all the way to his home, and watched as he parked and went inside.

CHAPTER 5

THE RINGING PHONE JERKED AVA VIOLENTLY OUT OF THE fitful sleep she'd fallen into after Ricky Don made his remark and walked out the door. She still felt hot all over every time she remembered what he'd said.

She never answered the house phone. She let Lynn's voice take the message. But it was a hang-up, just like all the others had been in the past few days. They came at all hours of the day or night. She'd forgotten to tell Ricky Don about them.

Ricky Don. She still thought it was a silly name. But now the sound of it didn't bring her to hysterical giggles. How had she come so far in such a few days? Had it only been a week? How could she change her mind about a person in such a short time? She was no different than those silly twits in the police department, acting all coy and "female" around him. Crap!

She needed to get off the sofa and go to bed, but she knew she wouldn't sleep in the bed any more than she was sleeping on the sofa. It seemed that sleep had left her for the time being.

Suddenly her brain shut down. Someone was gently turning the doorknob to the front door, as if they were testing to see if it would open. Back and forth. Slowly. Noiselessly.

Getting up from the sofa, Ava padded softly to the umbrella

47

stand that stood beside the door. She took out the oversized umbrella that Lynn insisted on using. Holding the pointed end, Ava drew back and slammed the wooden handle against the door about where she thought the person's head might be.

"Sonofabitch!" she heard a muffled male voice exclaim as footsteps ran down the sidewalk in hasty retreat.

"That's right. That's exactly what you are," she yelled at the door.

She went to her purse and took out her pepper spray, took a huge knife from the kitchen, and sat back down on the sofa. There would be no sleep tonight.

She should probably call Ricky Don just in case the door-knob tester came back, but he had run away like a scared coward, so maybe it was just someone looking for a random door to be unlocked, thereby offering easy pickings. She'd feel silly if there was nothing to it.

Plus she'd be in more danger from her own self if Ricky Don came back tonight. She had to get a grip on her feelings before she saw him again.

Instead she downloaded the data from Cloneall Drugs, Inc. from Yahoo! and spent the rest of the night going back over the data.

Occasionally the sound of approaching footsteps would startle her out of her concentration. Her heart would pound as she watched the doorknob, then she'd breath a sigh of relief when the person or persons walked on past to their own apartment.

As a tinge of light appeared behind the curtains Ava knew the sun would be coming up soon and she felt more secure. Overcome with exhaustion, she decided to go to bed and try to snatch a few hours of sleep before she started her day. *What day?* she wondered as she slipped into the first nightgown her hands fell on. As the sleek satin material slid over her body, she realized she'd picked up one of Lynn's ridiculous stand-ins for sleepwear. But too tired to care, she fell onto the bed without even turning the covers back and was sound asleep by the time her head hit the pillow.

RICKY DON MCKINZIE GLANCED UP FROM THE PAPERWORK that he'd been consumed with all morning. Eleven o'clock. He dialed Ava's cell phone for the fourth time that morning without getting an answer. The worry that had been nagging at him came to the front. He'd given her all the excuses she needed for not answering her phone. Now he was worried.

Pulling into the apartment complex, he saw Lynn's car sitting exactly where it had been last night when he left, so Ava must still be in the apartment. He dialed her phone again as he walked to the door. No answer.

Instead of knocking, he took the key that Lynn had given him and let himself in. The computer was on, but she wasn't anywhere around.

"Ava?" No answer.

With growing apprehension he checked the hall bathroom before making his way to the bedroom, where he stopped dead in his tracks.

Sunlight filtered through the curtains, casting a glow around a sleeping Ava. She was a picture straight out of a Rubens painting. In sleep, her defenses were gone. Her face was soft and almost cherubic. Her lips were slightly parted and had taken on a pouted look. His eyes continued to take in her dark hair against the white pillow, the lilac satin gown dipping low enough to expose ample cleavage that he'd never even gotten a glimpse of, and the curves she kept hidden under those loose T-shirts she insisted on wearing.

Feeling like a voyeur but not really caring, he eased into the chair beside her bed and watched her sleep.

What kind of woman was she, he wondered. She tried to be so tough when she was dealing with him, but could anyone who looked this innocent actually be all that tough? Was she guarding herself against something? Had she been hurt in the past? Who was she?

He didn't know yet, but sure planned to find out.

But he realized that sitting here watching the gentle rise and fall of her breasts as she breathed wasn't going to work. He'd better wake her up or he would wind up on the bed with her.

"Ava." He tried to keep his voice low and not startle her. "Ava," he said again, moving to the bedside and gently touching her arm.

"No!" she cried out, sitting straight up in bed. "No! Get away from me!"

"Ava! It's me. It's okay," he said, but backed away a little to give her space.

"Ricky Dick?" Sleep slowly left her as she gained consciousness.

Knowing that she didn't feel threatened anymore, Ricky Don leaned over and captured her sleep-swollen lips in his. Because he couldn't seem to resist since he'd had a taste of them, and because of the name she'd called him and the promise he'd made her.

He wasn't expecting her response. Still vulnerable from sleep, she forgot her defenses and instead leaned into the kiss as she slid a hand to his face. She'd wanted to touch his face ever since she'd seen him smile the first time. She was intrigued with the creases that bracketed his mouth when he smiled.

This was wonderful. So much more than she'd allowed herself to feel when he'd kissed her before. She'd never known that a simple kiss could make her go liquid all over. It had never happened before. And to think that it had to be Detective McKinzie who was doing this to her.

Ricky Dick? Shock brought her to her senses, and she quickly pushed back from him.

"What are you doing here? In this apartment? In the bed

with me? *What?*" Confusion, anger, and a touch of hysteria caused her voice to tremble.

Sliding his hands down her arms and gathering her hands in his, Ricky Don sat and watched the emotions play across her face. "You were enjoying the kiss. You can't deny that. What happened? Why did you suddenly become hysterical on me?"

"I'm not hysterical! It's just that you make me feel—you made me feel—"

"What, Ava? What do I make you feel?"

"That's just it," she whispered in a shaky voice. "You make me feel."

SHE'D PROMISED HERSELF AFTER HANK THAT SHE'D NEVER again allow anyone to get close enough to hurt her. She'd never allow anyone else to make her feel sexy. To feel loved and wanted. And then to be made to feel cheap, used, and thrown away. She never again wanted to go through the hurt. The anger. The bitterness that had followed Hank.

And here she sat on the side of Lynn's bed with a virtual stranger holding her hands and causing heat to boil her insides. Fighting the urge to lean into him and continue what he'd started, Ava stood and reached for a robe that hung on the back of the bedroom door.

"I'll make some coffee," she said as she headed for the kitchen.

AFTER THE COFFEE STARTED BREWING, AVA STOOD WITH BOTH hands on the counter and watched the water drip into the pot. Suddenly she couldn't face Ricky Don. She'd said too much in that one stuttering sentence, and now he'd want more. She could feel his eyes boring into her back as he sat at the small dinette table that was in the corner of the kitchen and patiently waited.

"Ava, come here. We've got to talk."

She sat down across from him. "Yes, we have to talk about what happened last night."

"Ava, last night we experienced and acknowledged a spark that we've both felt, just like we acknowledged it this morning. We're both adults. We're allowed to feel these things. And we can't just keep ignoring them. Or at least, I don't want to."

"I'm not talking about that. I'm talking about something that happened after you left."

The twinkling tease left his blue eyes and they suddenly became clouded with something she couldn't read. "What happened?"

"I was sitting there on the sofa and someone gently turned the doorknob several times, like they were testing to see if the door was unlocked."

"The sons of bitches! Okay, that does it. I'm going to be with you around the clock from now on."

He went to the coffee pot, filled two cups and brought them back to the table.

"Wait. Let me finish. I took Lynn's umbrella and hit the door and they cursed and ran away. I really feel like it was just someone who was hoping for a random unlocked door for easy pilfering. But I felt like I needed to let you know—just in case."

"Is that why you reacted like you did when I woke you up?"

"Probably. But I'm not used to having a man sitting on my bed when I wake up, so I don't know how I would react."

The teasing look was back in his eyes. "Well, I'd be happy to help you get used to having a man in bed with you."

The shield came over her eyes, totally closing herself off from him. "Been there, done that," she said, sipping her coffee.

"And you got hurt."

"And I got hurt."

"Well, whoever the asshole was that hurt you wasn't me. I don't hurt women, Ava."

"Look, we don't need to analyze me. We have more important things to think about than who I've shared my bed with or who I will or won't share it with in future."

As if making her point for her, the house phone rang. She waited for the caller to hang up, as she always did.

"Does that happen a lot?" Ricky Don asked.

"Several times a day."

"Do you check the caller ID?"

"It's always 'Unknown Name, Unknown Number.'"

"If it rings again while I'm here, I'll answer it. Maybe whoever it is needs to know there's a man around."

"I know it could be phone solicitors, but every time it rings I get a creepy feeling. But that's probably more my imagination than anything else."

"Probably not. I don't like it. It smells very suspicious."

The ringing of his cell phone interrupted them. Ava could tell it was the LAPD on the phone.

"I've got to go to the office," he said after completing the call. "After I finish questioning this suspect, I'll come back and get you and we'll go to your house and see if we can find some clue to help us. I've been over there several times, but can't find anything. But since you're more familiar with it you might see something I'm missing."

"Thank you. I think that would help me get a grip on all that's happened. What a difference a few days can make in a person's life."

"We'll get to the bottom of this. I promise you. I should be back in a couple of hours."

HE DIDN'T REMEMBER UNTIL HE WAS ALMOST TO THE STATION that he'd forgotten to ask why she didn't answer her phone. He dialed the number, but still no answer. But at least he knew she was okay for now.

Ava's first plan was to get a shower. As she left the living room she placed a dining room chair under the front doorknob, hoping it would slow down anyone who might try to force the door open. She was becoming paranoid, and she hated it.

As the hot water from the shower peppered her skin, she began to relax. What was she going to do about these feelings she was having for Ricky Don McKinzie? She had to find a way to deal with this situation. Had to find a way to stop her heart from pounding every time he got close.

She had promised herself she would never, *ever* get involved with a man again. The hurt just wasn't worth it. And there would be hurt. There was always hurt. She didn't believe that "happily ever after" applied to her.

There had been no happily ever after for her mom. The man who had fathered Ava had left the instant her mom told him she was pregnant. Ava had never seen him and never wanted to see him. Her mom had never tried to find love again. She hadn't been bitter against men; she just decided life was easier for her and Ava without one around.

Ava had always encouraged her mom to date, but it never happened. After Ava's encounter with Hank she understood her mom's position, and had adopted it for her own.

But now she wondered if her mom had ever been tempted with another man, like Ricky Don tempted her.

Temptation. That was the key word, right there. It was just lust and temptation, and she planned to nip that in the bud instantly!

After drying off she opened the door to Lynn's closet and stood staring at the expensive pantsuits, slacks, fancy blouses, tops, jackets and dresses. Rebellion suddenly rose up inside her. *Not today,* she thought.

Professor Lutz and his goons were turning her world upside down and she was getting really ready to right that wrong. Damn them anyway! Why did she have to change who she was just to avoid a bunch of hoodlums?

But remembering that she had agreed to go along with this

charade for a while, she took a pair of Lynn's dark-colored designer jeans and a red knit shirt that had small beads bordering the neckline. She tucked the shirt in and put on a short denim jacket. She'd seen Lynn wear this exact combination before, so it must be okay. She knew Lynn wouldn't have been seen in public if it didn't match. She smiled, thinking about her friend, and realized how much she missed her.

After putting on as little of the required makeup as possible, she went to the computer to do more research on the two sets of data. She still hadn't found out where the numbers had been changed to make the data say the direct opposite than it had said the first time.

She'd barely gotten into the database when the phone rang. She waited until the expected hang up, then went back to the data. But the phone rang again. Then again. After the fifth time exasperation took over her and she snatched the receiver off the hook and said, "What the hell do you want?"

"Ava?" Lynn's hesitant voice came from the other end of the line.

"Lynn! What are you doing calling this line? Why didn't you call my cell phone?"

"I did, but you haven't answered all morning, and I need you to do something for me if you have time."

"Okay, but let me check my cell phone and call you back."

Ava went to the bedside table and got her cell phone. It didn't take a minute to realize she'd let the battery run down. She did a quick charge and saw the missed calls from Ricky Don and Lynn.

She called Lynn back and explained what she'd done. "Oh, and he used the key you gave him to let himself in. I woke up and he was sitting on the bed beside me! You could have at least let me know you'd given him the key."

After Lynn had recovered from laughing, she asked, "Why did you answer the phone the way you did?"

"Because I always let the answering machine take the messages in your voice, and I've been getting a lot of hang up calls. Why didn't you leave a message? Or at lease say something so I'd know it was you."

"Because I knew I shouldn't call that number, and was afraid the wrong person might hear me if they have it bugged. Since you weren't answering your cell phone I kind of panicked. I should have known you had let the battery run down. You always do that, you know. But while we're under these circumstances, please try to remember to keep it charged, okay?" Fear and concern for her best friend caused Lynn's voice to tremble.

"Lynn, I'm okay. I'm going to be okay. You don't have to worry," Ava admonished. "So what do you need for me to do?"

"I have to renew my driver's license before next month and I forgot to bring my renewal letter and information with me. Will you mail that to me so I can take care of it online?"

"No problem. I'll put that in the mail today. Where is it?"

"It's in the car, in the glove compartment. I carried it there, thinking I'd run by the DMV one day and take care of it. But then I wound up here without it." After chatting a few more minutes, they hung up.

Ava headed for the car to get the information Lynn needed. She'd get it ready to mail so she and Ricky Don could drop it off at the post office on the way to her house.

Although she dreaded going back into her house and seeing the damage that had been done, she was excited about possibly finding some incriminating clue that could be used against Professor Lutz. She was about to open the door of Lynn's Cadillac when she saw the flat tire. *Crap! What did I run over to cause that tire to go flat?* she wondered.

Leaning over to inspect it, she saw the large slash in the tire. A deep, nasty gash ran across the front right side. After a quick inspection, she found all four tires in the same shape. Someone had slit all her tires.

CHAPTER 6

AVA REACHED INTO THE GLOVE COMPARTMENT TO GET Lynn's driver's license renewal letter and at the same time noticed a folded note tucked under the windshield wiper.

Making sure the car doors were locked, she took the note and went back inside her apartment and quickly locked the door behind her. Who had slashed the tires and left the note? Was it the same person who had tried her doorknob last night?

Dread coursed through her as she slowly unfolded the note. *Answer your phone or the next thing to go will be the windshield.*

As if on cue the phone rang. Surely it wasn't the person who wrote the note. They couldn't know she had it, could they? Not wanting to take the chance, Ava snatched the phone up and said, "What?"

"Good girl. You learn fast. Now you do this every time and we won't have to hurt that nice car of yours anymore. The car or—anything else." The voice was barely above a whisper, scratchy with an otherworldly sound.

Cold fear washed over Ava. She recognized the "anything else" for the personal threat that it was. But they thought they were threatening Lynn—didn't they? And if so, why? Were they going to intimidate Lynn to try and get to her?

She also knew now that they were watching her. They were watching the apartment. They knew when she came and went. That's why there was never a hang up call on the caller ID when she had left the apartment for some reason. They knew when she was there and when she wasn't. Did they follow her when she left the apartment?

For the first time since she'd met him, she needed Ricky Don McKinzie. She needed him with her. She wanted him with her. And that fact bothered her way more than she wanted to admit.

Whoever was watching her also knew when Ricky Don came and went. *Do they know who he is?* The thought flashed into her mind, unwanted.

The ringing of her cell phone startled her. Glancing at the caller ID, she saw that it was Ricky Don. "I'm walking to your door," he said. "Do you want me to let myself in?"

"No! Hold on and let me open the door for you," she answered. He'd only used the key once that she was aware of, so maybe the watchers hadn't seen him. They didn't need to know he could come and go as he pleased.

She had the door open as he approached. He reached for her, but she grabbed his arm and quickly pulled him inside.

"Well, now, that's even more than I'd hoped for," he drawled. "Just can't wait for me to get inside, huh?" And he reached for her.

"Wait! We've got to talk. Do you want some coffee?"

"Sure, I'll take some coffee. What's goin' on? You seem jumpy."

"They're watching me," she said, handing him a mug of steaming coffee. "They're watching the apartment. They know when I come and when I go. They know when *you* come and when you go. That's why I didn't want you to use the key."

"How do you know this?" He'd suddenly lost interest in his coffee and set the mug on the dinette table where he'd eased into a chair.

Sitting down opposite him, she told him about the slashed tires, the note and the phone call. "I wonder if they know who you are," she said.

Again as if on cue, the phone rang. "Put it on speaker phone so I can hear the voice," Ricky Don said.

"Tell your friend we said 'hello,'" the weird voice whispered. Then the phone went dead.

"They're messing with your mind," Ricky Don said. "They're talkin' through a machine that distorts their voice. It sounds like they're usin' a mic and amplifier like some singers use to change the sound of their voice."

"But if they think I'm Lynn, what purpose do they think it will serve to intimidate me?"

"I'm sure they'll let you know when they're ready to make their move."

"Do you think they know who you are?"

"That's another thing we'll have to wait and find out."

"How long do we wait? Do I just sit here until someone tries to kill me again? No! I won't be a sitting duck! This is getting me no closer to finding out what Cloneall Drugs and Professor Lutz are up to."

"Maybe they're waiting to see if you're goin' to blow the whistle on them."

"Then maybe I should go ahead and do it. I've been going over the data, trying to find where the numbers were changed, but every time I get into it I get interrupted. Maybe I'll sit up all night and look for it tonight."

"Let me know when you find it. I have a friend at the LAPD who can give us some advice on how to go forward. I'm thinkin' you need a very good lawyer before you do anything else."

Ava had relaxed just knowing that Ricky Don was with her. She watched expressions cross his face and flicker different degrees of blue flashes from his eyes. In just a few short weeks she'd gone from laughing at him hysterically to being lulled by his Southern drawl. In fact, she was beginning to feel warm sparks shoot through her every time his sultry voice dropped a "g."

Shocked at the turn of her thoughts, she quickly snapped herself out of them and suggested, "Shouldn't we leave? I need to run by the post office and put Lynn's letter in the mail before we head over to my house." Turning off the coffee pot, she started gathering up the things she needed to take with her.

Ricky Don's hand covered hers as she started to pick up her purse. "Are you okay? You sure went into action quickly. Is there somethin' you're not tellin' me?"

Yeah, like maybe you're beginning to really turn me on? "No, I just want to get away from the apartment for a while. I can't stand the thought of someone watching where I am, even if they can't see me."

AVA STOOD, STUNNED, AS RICKY DON PULLED THE CURTAINS open at each window and allowed light to shine on the ugly truth of what had been done to her home. Because she'd been so upset the day she'd found Lynn lying in a pool of blood, she hadn't comprehended the chaos that had been wrought on her belongings. The only other time she'd been back the house had been dark inside.

Her first impulse was to sink down onto the sofa and try to take it all in, but the cushions had been destroyed by knife slashes and the insides dug out and strewn over the floor.

Porcelain figurines that had been her mom's were broken into pieces too small to ever be put back together. Cuddles, the stuffed dog her mom had paid to have made specifically for her, lay ripped and destroyed, the head angled, almost totally torn from the body.

She was convinced whoever did this was looking for the data, but half of the broken items were too small to hide anything in, much less a storage device. Those things were broken just for the sake of doing it. Whoever had done this had a real mean streak.

She didn't realize tears were flowing down her face until Ricky Don came to her and pulled her to him. "Let it out, baby," he said, wrapping her in his arms.

And she did. She buried her face in his shoulder and let the tears flow. Tears for Lynn, tears for her home, and tears for Mike.

Ricky Don's voice soothed while she wept. His words didn't register through the thoughts that crowded her mind and fed her tears, but his voice was there. Calm. Gentle. Encouraging her to feel what she felt and let it out.

As the tears slowly subsided, Ava pulled back from him and said, "Okay, what am I allowed to touch? To move? Do I have to leave everything exactly as it is?"

Reluctantly, he let her slip out of his arms. "For now, we'd better just look and not disturb too much. We're still tryin' to find some link to who may have done this."

Resigned to leave everything that had been her life lying in ruin, Ava started slowly moving over each inch of the living room. Somewhere there had to be a clue that would lead them to Professor Lutz. She had no doubt that he had been behind this.

Without being aware of the passing of time, she picked up each item and looked at it and under it, being careful to place it back just like it had been. She spent time on her knees, time standing, time bending over. Searching. Hoping. Waiting. Time silently mourning *her* stuff that had been destroyed. Time in which a growing anger boiled inside her.

Across the room, Ricky Don was searching every inch of that side.

For long periods of time no words were spoken. None were needed.

Ava sat on the floor, going through a stack of utility bills that had been swiped off her desk and scattered on the floor. Glancing quickly through them, she knew they'd all been paid, since she had them automatically deducted from her bank account. That way she didn't have to worry about being late; she just had to worry about having money in the bank to cover the bills. She had enough in her checking account to cover a few more months, but unless she went to work soon, that would be gone.

She was about to give up on finding anything when she picked up the last bill on the floor and realized a small piece of paper was clinging to the back of the envelope. Almost discarding it as nothing, she glanced at it and realized the writing on the paper wasn't hers. Looking closer, she saw that it was a phone number she didn't recognize.

"Ricky Don, I think I have something," she said, barely above a whisper. "This isn't my handwriting and it's not a number I recognize, so the people who were in here must have dropped it. Unless one of the investigating officers dropped it."

He took the slip of paper she handed him and studied it. "I think the best thing we can do is run a computer search and see if it leads us to a location. If it's listed, we should be able to get an address from a search engine. I can also ask around to see if any of the officers who were here recognize it. One of them may have dropped it."

"Or we could find a pay phone and just call the number. That would save a lot of trouble if it's a dead end," Ava suggested.

"That's actually a great idea. I like the way you think. Would you consider being my partner on the force?"

"Nah. Too much drama for me."

"And being chased by a bunch of crazies isn't drama?"

"Case in point. But my drama will be over soon and I can forget about it. You'll always be involved with the next case, so you won't ever be free of it. I don't think I would want to live like that."

"Even as the wife of a police officer?"

The question took them both by surprise. Eyes locked as they stared at each other for the space of an entire minute.

"Well, since I can't see that ever happening, I guess we should go call this number," Ava said. "But before we leave I'd like to check out the bedrooms. I haven't been in them since this whole thing happened."

Ricky Don took hope in the fact that she hadn't dogmatically said that being a policeman's wife would never happen. He watched her hips swing from the room and grinned. What a woman! He'd never met a woman like Ava Manning, and he liked everything about her.

But did he like her enough to try to make a life with her? Was he falling in love with her? What had prompted him to say what he'd said? And why had it mattered that she hadn't turned him down point blank?

Ava stood staring at her bedroom. It was in worse shambles than the living room.

"I was hopin' you wouldn't want to look in here," Ricky Don said from behind her.

"So you've already seen it?"

"Yes. I, and the other investigatin' officers, have been through the entire house. The other bedroom and both baths have been junked, too. They may have just wanted to steal your computer and make this look like a robbery, but they wanted to make sure you hadn't hidden a copy of that data somewhere else. These folks mean business, Ava."

"I know. They tried to kill me. And they did kill Mike. They mean business, alright."

"I'm real worried about you stayin' in Lynn's apartment, now that we know they're watchin' it. I don't want you there. I think you should come and stay with me until this is over."

"No."

"No? Just like that? Why not?"

"Because I think we're better off with them thinking they're close to me. If I leave, then they'll try to find me. If they know I'm at the apartment they'll continue to watch it, and maybe that will lull them into not watching other things that we're doing."

"Reluctantly, I agree. Again, I like the way you think. Okay. So I'll come and stay with you."

"Ricky Di—Don, you can't be with me all the time! So there's no use in you staying with me. It would only be at night anyway, since you have to work during the day."

He patiently waited until she finished, then captured her lips in a long, slow kiss.

"That's for almost calling me the wrong name," he said.

"That's not fair!" she protested, after gaining control of her breath. "I changed it and didn't finish saying Ricky Dick."

Cupping her chin in his hand, Ricky Don pulled her close again. This time the kiss was longer, slower and more intense.

"And that was just because I wanted to," he said, covering her lips again.

Their breathing became one, and Ava could only cling to him as heat coursed through her body. Nobody had ever made her feel like this. Not even Hank, when she thought she was really in love with him.

Because her reactions panicked her, Ava pulled away from Ricky Don and stepped back.

He let her go because he recognized that she was running from her own feelings. Not him. He could feel her response to him. Her quickening pulse. Her flushed face. But he knew she had to work through whatever was in her past that haunted her.

"Let's go make that phone call," he said, kissing her another quick time.

WORKING PAY PHONES WERE GETTING HARDER AND HARDER to find in the wake of cell phones that most people now carried. But eventually they found one, and Ricky Don handed Ava the money while she dialed the number.

After the phone rang several times a voice answered, and Ava hung the receiver up with a bang.

"What?" Ricky Don asked.

"Mike answered the phone," she said. All color had drained from her face as she stared at Ricky Don.

"But he's dead," Ricky Don said.

"He's supposed to be dead, but that was him on the phone. I'd bet my life on it."

CHAPTER 7

"**H**OW CAN YOU BE SO SURE? YOU DIDN'T EVEN KNOW THAT was his number. Why didn't you know that was his phone number? I thought you were friends."

"We were work acquaintances, not friends like hanging out together or calling each other after work hours. I had no reason to ever call him at home. But Mike had a distinct voice. It was like it was hung somewhere between his child voice and the puberty-voice-changing stage. It hung on certain words, causing him to sound like he was trying to yodel, kind of like Mr. Haney on that old TV show, *Green Acres*. I would know that voice anywhere. His voice always sounds like it cracks and goes up a notch when he says "hello,' and that's what just happened."

"But that was him you identified at the morgue, wasn't it?"

"I'd bet my life on that, too. I don't know what's going on, but that was Mike at the morgue and that was Mike's voice on the phone."

"Do you know where he lived?" Ricky Don asked.

"I don't know the exact location, but he rented a small apartment close to the beach, he said."

"I'll do a search on this phone number when I get back to

the office and see if I can find the exact location. Then we'll stake it out and see who's goin' and comin' from the address."

WHILE DRIVING BACK TO LYNN'S APARTMENT, RICKY DON called a garage service and made arrangements for them to come out and put new tires on Lynn's Cadillac. As soon as he had made sure Ava was safely in the apartment, he met the mechanics out front and stood with them while they replaced the tires.

Ava watched him from the front window of the apartment. She knew he was casually watching for any van-type vehicle or an apartment where the people watching her might be. She'd stood at the window and searched for the same thing on several occasions. But there was nothing she could find that was out of the ordinary.

After Ricky Don and the mechanics had left, she sat on the sofa and steamed over the situation. How much longer? Their progress seemed as flat as the four slashed tires that had just been hauled off.

As an idea formed in her head, her heart rate jumped into high gear. She knew exactly what she would do while she was "waiting." Tomorrow she would call Carlotta, the head supervisor of the cleaning crew at the lab. She knew for a fact that Carlotta hated Professor Lutz. He'd been verbally abusive to her on many occasions, and had made clear his disdain for her Mexican heritage. He thought she needed her job too badly to report him for harassment. And besides that, he was *Professor Lutz,* as he'd pointed out to her on a day when he'd been complaining about the way the lab was cleaned. Who would believe a *Mexican* over a *professor,* he'd asked her, with pure contempt steeped in every word.

But she wouldn't make that call from the apartment. Not on the house phone, for sure, and not even on her cell phone, because they might even be able to tap into the signal. She'd make the call tomorrow when she went to Costumes For The Occasion.

Excitement filled Ava as her plan took place. A plan she wouldn't tell Ricky Don about, because she was sure he'd try to put a stop to it before it even got off the ground. Nope. This was something she would do, then tell him after the fact, if necessary.

No thought crossed her mind as to the safety of what she was planning. She knew it was a foolproof plan and she was determined to go forward with it.

With the confidence of a well-laid plan and the stirring excitement that went with it, Ava was sure she wouldn't be able to sleep anytime soon. So she went to the computer and continued her search for the data that had been tampered with.

"You know that if they discover you helped me with this, you'll lose your job," Ava said to the short, plump Mexican woman sitting across the table from her at an outside café on a side of town Professor Lutz wouldn't have been caught dead in.

"Do you have any idea how much I hate that man?" Carlotta asked. "He has talked to me like I'm a dog on every occasion he can find. I'm honored to help you take him down! The cleaning service can't please the man. He finds something wrong with our work every single night. It's obvious that he looks down his educated, pompous nose at us peons."

"So I'll just show up every night and work from 12:00 to 6:00 a.m. as if I'm one of your crew. The rest of the cleaning crew won't know that I'm not actually on payroll or that you didn't run a background check on me."

"That's right. Who's going to ask a question like that anyway? It's none of their business, and they'll be happy to have extra help."

"I'd just feel horrible if you lost your job over this."

"Get real, Ava. I can get another job cleaning buildings. And after you told me about what they're doing to you, it's worth losing my job if you can stop what they're trying to do. You've always been nice to me. You've always treated me as an equal, and that means a lot to me."

"Well, you *are* an equal, Carlotta. You're a human being just like I am. What we do for a living doesn't make us better or worse than someone else."

They stood and hugged each other goodbye. "I'll see you tonight, cleaning lady," Carlotta said.

"Lady?" Ava asked, and smiled as Carlotta walked away, laughing.

AVA HAD NEVER RECEIVED A PHONE CALL AFTER 10:00 P.M. from the people watching her at Lynn's apartment. She'd often wondered if they went home at night or just went to sleep. But she couldn't take a chance on any cameras they might have that could catch her if she left the apartment.

She maneuvered Lynn's Cadillac through the LA traffic back to the apartment. She'd developed the habit of taking side streets and different directions when she came and went, just in case they were following her. She'd also developed the habit of keeping an eye on her rearview mirror. Occasionally she'd spot a black van a few cars behind her. When she did, she'd immediately take a side street.

But today she hadn't seen anything suspicious. That made her more nervous than when she thought she'd seen them.

She'd received fewer calls this week, also. Maybe they were convinced she was going to answer the phone now, so they didn't bother. But she knew they hadn't gone away. She could feel eyes on her every time she came and went from the apartment. And she felt them today as she made her way up the sidewalk to the apartment.

AT 11:00 P.M., AVA STOOD IN FRONT OF LYNN'S FULL-LENGTH mirror and stared at the stranger looking back at her. The figure had a full beard, bushy eyebrows, and a baseball cap perched on its head. Denim coveralls and a plaid shirt covered a rounded stomach and slouched haphazardly over a pair of motorcycle boots.

Ava adjusted the pillow she had tied around her midriff, to make sure it fit snugly under her boobs to blend in and look like a natural stomach. Everything except the boots had come from Costumes For The Occasion.

Satisfied with the results, she was sure nobody would ever recognize her. She tucked her driver's license, her cell phone and a few dollars into the pockets of the coveralls, and went out through the back door of the apartment.

She'd have to walk about half a block to get to the end of the apartment building, but then she could cut through and go back for her bike. She hoped Mr. Bigg and his goons hadn't paid any attention to the bike, which had sat untouched since she'd been at Lynn's. Hopefully they didn't have a clue it would be anywhere around, even if they knew it was her normal mode of transportation.

Trying to walk casually, she finally made her way to the bike. Thankfully it started on the first try, and she eased slowly out of the apartment complex, willing the bike to be as quiet as a Harley could be. When she got to the street she pumped the gas and felt the thrill of finally being back on the love of her life. Even with the beard and extra clothing keeping the full impact of the night wind from her, she felt the thrill.

She was sorry when she made it to Cloneall Drugs and had to park the bike and go inside.

Glancing around, she spotted a red Mustang a few spaces from where she'd parked. Without thinking she stopped in mid-stride and stared at the car to see if it was Ricky Don McKinzie. And he was staring back at her as if trying to figure out who she was.

Crap! Had he recognized her bike? No! There were too many bikes just like hers for him to know one from the other. Still, he did know his vehicles. Shrugging her shoulders, she headed for the entrance. She couldn't worry about that now. She had a lab to clean and some nosing around to do.

But what was he doing here?

RICKY DON PUT MIKE CAMPBELL'S PHONE NUMBER IN Google search and came up with an address for Mack Campbell. Mack? Mike? That was interesting.

After working after hours on another case file, he decided to go and watch the Campbell address for a while. Maybe he'd get lucky. He found the address, but knew from the looks of the upscale apartments that this wasn't a "cheap apartment close to the beach" like Ava had thought. Maybe this Mike/Mack thing was just a coincidence, but he found an inconspicuous spot and settled in for the wait. He couldn't be where he wanted to be, anyway, which was with Ava, so he might as well be on stakeout.

He didn't have to ask what it was about her that caused his blood to boil. He'd seen women he was attracted to, and being a normal all-American boy he'd had his share of them. But it was always on the mutual agreement that nothing was to come of the flings. He wanted to settle down and get married some day, but in his mind "some day" was a long way off from this day. Suddenly, though, it didn't seem so far away.

Now he frequently found his mind wandering into the future when it came to this big beautiful goddess. He smiled at the name he'd secretly started calling her. What would his 110-pound mom think when he introduced Ava to her? Not that he thought his mom would be judgmental, but Ava was just her opposite. His mother was the June Cleaver of her time. She was content to let his dad make most of the decisions for the home, although she could and would jump in and make her opinion known if she needed to.

See? Here he was doing it again. Already introducing Ava to his parents and wondering how they would accept her. He'd never even asked Ava for a date, for Pete's sake! And he fully doubted she'd go if he did. Although she did seem to enjoy his kisses.

Just the thought of how her body pressed against his and how soft and yielding her lips were caused pain to shoot through his lower body.

But he'd have to get past the man or person who had hurt her. He could tell it was hard for her to trust him. He didn't think it was just him. She wasn't ready to trust her heart to any man. Yet.

Better change the thought pattern, he admonished himself, just as someone walked out of the apartment he was watching.

Someone who looked just like the corpse Ava had identified as Mike Campbell.

Ricky Don glanced at his watch. 10:30.

The look-alike climbed into an old Jaguar and shot the gas, leaving so fast that Ricky Don almost lost him. He managed to catch up and followed the car to Cloneall Drugs.

He pulled in a parking space and watched as the Mike Campbell look-alike strolled into the building as if he knew exactly where he was going.

What was going on? Had the body that had washed ashore that looked like Mike Campbell been a coincidence? But why did Mike Campbell's phone number lead to a Mack Campbell's apartment?

This case was getting more complicated each day, with no answers showing up. Just the kind of case Ricky Don McKinzie loved. But he knew he had to make progress because of Ava's safety.

He was about to leave when a Harley growled to a stop a

few spaces from where he was parked. That sure looked like Ava's bike. But a bearded man stepped off the bike and started toward the building, then turned quickly and looked directly at him.

Do I know you? Ricky Don wondered. *You sure look like you know me.* But the guy shrugged and made his way into the building.

Ricky Don decided the night air was getting to him. He needed to go home and try to get some sleep.

CHAPTER 8

"**M**R. SMITH?" CARLOTTA ASKED, LOOKING CLOSELY AT Ava as she approached.

"Yes," Ava answered in her deepest voice. Since she had a naturally husky voice, it was fairly easy to lower it to sound enough like a man's voice to get by with. She'd never be able to sing bass, but it was good enough.

"I'm so glad you could make it," Carlotta replied, then went into a peal of laughter that Ava was sure would alert the entire building. Carlotta ducked into the ladies' room that she'd just finished cleaning, and continued to laugh until she got control of herself.

Ava had brought a small portable CD player with a headset to wear while she cleaned. She wasn't listening to anything, but wanted it to appear that she was so she could eavesdrop on any conversation around her while looking as if she wasn't paying any attention. Occasionally, when she remembered, she'd bob her head as if a song was playing that she really liked.

As she mopped her way through the corridor she came to the lab where she'd worked. She casually looked around to see if anyone was watching her, and gently tried to open the door. It was locked. Hmm. That was strange. Who would be here at this time of night? She tried again, but nothing happened.

She continued to mop her way to the end of the corridor, where she stopped and waited. If someone were in the lab, they'd have to come out that door when they left. She'd make sure she kept an eye on the door.

But by the time for her to stop work, nobody had ventured out the lab door. So if someone had been in there, how did they get out? Unless—unless they were still in the lab.

Did she dare hang around and watch? No. She would be too conspicuous.

TWO WEEKS HAD PASSED SINCE AVA HAD STARTED HER disguised cleaning job. Two weeks of backbreaking work. Two weeks of finding a locked lab door each night. Two weeks of total frustration.

She had no way of knowing that each time she tried the lab door, two heads inside the room had turned to look at it. And she had no way of knowing that in the wee hours of the morning two figures slipped silently out through an emergency side door that exited the room.

The emergency alarm had been deactivated from the door, so nobody knew when it was opened. The security guard who watched the monitors by night was being paid handsomely to look the other way.

FOR SURE, AVA HAD GAINED A NEW RESPECT FOR PEOPLE WHO worked in the housekeeping industry. It was very hard work, but gradually it was becoming easier.

Her days had fallen into a routine. Each night at 7:00 she went to bed to try and get some sleep before getting up at 11 P.M. to go to work. Then when she got home at 6:30 in the morning, she would lie back down and try to get a few more hours of sleep.

All of this depended on when or if Ricky Don called with some thought or question about the case. Usually she would arrange to meet him during the middle of the day, but she didn't know how much longer she could keep coming up with excuses to not meet him or let him come over before midday.

Somehow she found time each day to go through small sections of the data, but couldn't find even a clue as to where the changes had been made.

She'd had a very close call with Ricky Don tonight. He'd insisted on coming over with pizza and wine, and had stayed until almost time for her to get dressed for work.

But after multiple genuine yawns, he'd gotten the message and stood to leave. "Soon, Ava, you're going to have to let me spend the night here," he'd said, pulling her close and kissing her, as had become his custom each time they were together.

After her heart had settled down from triple-beat, she started putting on her costume.

With another huge yawn, she knew tonight would be hell. She should just call Carlotta and tell her she was staying home. It's not like she was getting paid to do this work. But just as sure as she didn't go, this would be the night she might be able to get into the lab. Sooner or later that door would be left unlocked.

She checked the mirror to make sure her disguise was in place and was about to pick up the keys to the motorcycle when she heard a hard pounding on the front door.

She froze. Now what? She couldn't go to the door dressed like this. But if it was Ricky Don, he knew she was inside and he'd use his key to get in if she didn't answer.

As she stood staring at the door trying to decide what to do, she heard the key turn slowly in the lock.

Panicking, she quickly ducked into the hall closet to hide, but left the door cracked just enough to see who was coming into the apartment.

"She's here," she heard Ricky Don say as he pushed the door open. "I haven't been gone but 20 minutes. I came back for my cell phone. I forgot it when I left."

Ava hadn't even noticed he'd forgotten it, but before she could get that thought into her mind Lynn walked through the door, followed by Ricky Don, who called, "Ava! You have company."

"Lynn!" Ava yelped, jumping from the closet, forgetting about her disguise.

"What the hell?" Ricky Don said, and reached for the Kel-Tec .32-caliber automatic he kept in his pants pocket as a backup. "Freeze!" he demanded, pointing the gun at Ava, who remembered at that moment what she looked like.

"Oh, relax, Ricky Dick, it's me," she said, pulling off the ballcap and exposing her hair at the same time as she removed the beard, then running to Lynn to wrap her in a tight hug.

"What the hell are you doing in that?" Ricky Don asked. "Wait a minute. I've seen you in that getup somewhere."

"At the lab," Ava said. "Lynn, what are you doing here?" she asked, turning her back on Ricky Don, who at the time was being a nuisance with his questions. "Come over here and sit and let me look at you. Wait a minute, you can't be here! What are you doing here?"

"Quiet!" Ricky Don barked.

As both women turned to him, he said, "Okay, it seems we all have some questions that need to be answered. Why don't we just sit down and go over them all, one by one."

"I'll make some coffee," Ava said. "This may take a while. Lynn, have you had dinner?"

"Yes, I'm fine," Lynn said, sitting on the sofa and looking around the apartment. "Wow. It's so good to see my stuff," she whispered.

Ava turned from the coffee pot straight into Ricky Don's arms and lips. "The name's Ricky Don," he reminded her after an extended kiss.

"Don't even ask," Ava said to Lynn, who was staring at them

with a stunned look on her face. Ava sat down on the couch beside her. "Now, what are you doing here?"

"Well—"

"Oh, wait a minute! I've got to make a phone call." Ava pulled her cell phone out of one of the side pockets of her coveralls. "Nope. Better not do that. Ricky *Don,* may I use your phone for a second?"

"Why?" he asked.

"In case my service has been tapped into. I don't want anyone to know about the number I'm going to call."

"You will explain later," he said, handing her his phone. It was a statement, not a question.

Ava dialed Carlotta's phone number as she walked back into the kitchen. "Carlotta, I won't be there tonight. I've had something come up."

"Are you sick?" Carlotta's concerned voice asked.

"No, I'm okay. I just have unexpected company," she answered.

"Well, our favorite person just went—"

"Carlotta! No names, please. No details. Can you explain in code?"

"Our favorite person just went into the lab," Carlotta answered. " And there was someone with him. I heard the door lock behind them."

"I just *knew* someone was in there! I could almost feel them!" Ava could feel the frustration sweep over her. "But how did you see them tonight, when we haven't been seeing them before?"

"I came in early to do some paperwork that I didn't get done last night. They got here thirty minutes before we usually show up for work. But Ava—" Carlotta paused for a long few seconds.

"What, Carlotta? What's wrong?"

"Ava, the other person? He looked a lot like your surfer friend."

"What? Are you sure?"

"I'd bet my life on it. Ava, something bad is going on here. You have to be really careful."

"Okay. Okay. Look, let's don't say anymore on the phone. We'll talk more tomorrow. I have to go now," Ava said, watching Ricky Don impatiently roam around the apartment.

"So, okay, Lynn, you were saying why you came back," Ava said, handing Ricky Don's phone back to him and sitting back down on the couch.

"Not so fast," he interrupted her. "We have all night to hear Lynn's story. Right now I want to hear what you're up to."

"We have just as long to hear mine as we do Lynn's. I want her to go first."

"Ava, you're pushing your luck with me. I smell danger in what you're doing, and I need to know right now what this is all about."

Ava realized she really liked seeing Ricky Don a little frustrated. But at this point he seemed more than a little frustrated, so she'd better come clean or she'd never find out why Lynn had suddenly shown up.

"I love it when you're pushy," she smiled, openly taunting him.

"You ain't seen pushy, woman. Talk to me."

"I'm working at the lab with the cleaning crew."

"Why?"

"I'm tired of waiting for the slow wheels of justice to make their way through the red tape. I want to get to the bottom of this case so all of our lives can get back to normal."

"But laws are made to be followed," Ricky Don patiently explained. "And you sound like I'm not doing all I can to get this case solved. Do you think you can do better?"

"Yep."

"You're deliberately making me crazy. Start from the beginning and tell me what's going on."

So Ava did exactly that. Ending with, "Carlotta saw two people go into the lab tonight. One was Professor Lutz, and she said the other one looked like Mike."

CHAPTER 9

"T HE PERSON SHE SAW THAT LOOKS LIKE MIKE ACTUALLY is the person you knew as Mike," Ricky Don said.

"What? But Mike's dead! I saw him in the morgue! I went to his funeral."

"You're right. Mike is dead. And you saw all the things you mentioned. But his identical twin brother, Mack, is who you knew as Mike."

"What?" Ava and Lynn echoed.

"Mike Campbell was born severely retarded. He spent most of his life in a mental institution. The information that I've been able to find indicates his brain didn't develop correctly while in the womb. Mack Campbell, Mike's identical twin, was and is highly intelligent. It's almost like he got both their brains.

"Their mother had them out of wedlock, and was a drunk and drug addict until she died when they were very young. Her parents wound up with custody of the boys, but they couldn't look after Mike in his condition, so they put him in Helping Hands, a local state-assisted institution, and raised Mack as their own child.

"But on a regular basis they would take Mack to visit his

brother. Mike adored Mack, and after they became adults Mack kept visitin' Mike, and would take him out of the institution occasionally for long rides or even overnight visits.

"But accordin' to Dr. Homer Cochran, the head director of the institution, it seems a couple of years ago, after their grandmother died, Mack decided to take total custody of Mike. He made all the arrangements to become Mike's guardian."

"And he was allowed to do that?" Ava asked.

"Yes. There was nothin' that could be done for Mike's mental health and he was in good health otherwise, so nothin' was keepin' him in the institution except their grandparents' signature. Since Mack was Mike's brother and both grandparents were dead, Mack became Mike's legal guardian. But he left Mike at the institution until a few months ago, when he came and took him for a visit and never brought him back."

"But how did Mike wind up dead on the beach?" Ava asked.

"That's what we're lookin' into. Mike's death was never reported to the institution. They still believed Mike was with Mack."

"So when were you going to let me in on all this information?" Ava asked. "Here I am, totally frustrated because nothing's happening on the case, and you've turned up a major finding."

"I was at the institution today, and found out for sure that they didn't know about Mike's death. I was goin' to tell you everything tonight, but you seemed so tired that I decided to let you get some rest and tell you tomorrow. But I guess you were fakin' the tiredness so you could rush off to do your own undercover work."

Ava felt the sting in Ricky Don's voice, but refused to feel guilty about what she was doing.

"Okay, so maybe we both need to be more honest with each other from now on, huh?" she offered as a consensus.

"Maybe. If you'll agree to quit your job."

"Why would I do that? I'm in a perfect place to eavesdrop on Klutz and Mi—Mack, or to check out the lab if I can ever get inside. No. I'm not going to quit."

"Ava, think about this. How long do you think it will take for the guys watchin' you to realize you're not here at night? Sooner or later one of them will call and you won't answer. Then they'll start watchin' you more closely and will find out what you're doin'. I really want you to stay away from the lab."

"I hate to interrupt the two of you, but may I throw out a suggestion?" Lynn had watched the interplay between her best friend and Ricky Don. Something had changed between them while she'd been gone. She had a lot of questions for Ava.

"Oh, Lynn. I'm sorry we're ignoring you," Ava said.

"Quite all right. But Ricky Don, I think Ava has a point. I'm worried about her, too, but with me being here, if one of the bad boys calls or comes to the door, they won't know any difference."

"No!" Ava and Ricky Don chorused.

"And, by the way, why are you back?" Ricky Don asked.

"I was beginning to feel in the way. Look, my parents were happy to see me, but they have their own routine. So after my extended visit, they needed to get back to that routine."

"Did they ask you to leave?" Ava asked.

"Heavens, no! My parents would never do that. I would be welcome there for life, if I needed to be there. It's just that I was beginning to feel uncomfortable. You know, kind of in the way? Anyway, I wanted to come home and check on things, so here I am."

"And that's the bottom line, I'm sure. You wanted to be here in the middle of everything, didn't you?" Ava jokingly accused.

"Kind of. I felt like you were having all the fun."

"Did you forget about the lick you got on your head? Was that fun to you?" Ricky Don asked. "Ladies, this is serious. Now I'll have two women to worry about instead of one."

"Well, aren't you just the male chauvinist pig!" Ava sputtered.

"And I'll amen that!" Lynn agreed.

"Okay. Okay. I know that wasn't politically correct, but I was raised in the South, dammit. I'm supposed to take care of ladies!"

"Why, Mistah McKinzie, suh! I'm so happy that we have y'all heah to take care of us!"

Ava bent double laughing at Lynn's perfect Southern accent. She often forgot her best friend was just as Southern as Ricky Don. Lynn had deliberately weeded out her accent, while Ricky Don seemed to emphasize his.

"Look, it's gettin' late. I have an early appointment in the mornin', and I know you two will be up half the night catchin' up with each other, so I'm headin' out. But I want to talk to both of you tomorrow. How about I bring pizza over for lunch, and we'll decide what to do about the two of you?"

"Oh, he just keeps gettin' more charmin' all the time, doesn't he?" Ava said to Lynn.

But before Lynn could answer, Ricky Don caught Ava's face between his hands and kissed her slowly. "Good night, ladies. I'll see y'all tomorrow," he said, and left.

"Girlfriend, sit down and talk to me! What's going on between you two? I haven't seen this many sparks fly since the Fourth of July," Lynn said, patting the couch beside her.

"Okay, but let me get out of these clothes first."

"I thought you looked nice," Lynn said. "Kind of normal."

"Shut up," Ava said, heading to the bedroom to change.

Lynn laughed as the two slipped instantly back into their comfortable routine.

RICKY DON WAS RIGHT. AVA AND LYNN TALKED AND LAUGHED until the wee hours of the morning.

Ava filled Lynn in on all that had gone on while she was

away, including how her feelings were changing about Ricky Don. She shared with Lynn how scared she was to open her heart and chance getting it broken all over again. Lynn knew Ava's history with Hank.

Lynn filled Ava in on all the fun she'd had catching up with old friends. She'd loved having long talks with her parents, one on one and individually. But she'd missed Ava and LA, so she'd decided to take her chances and come back.

She'd left Kibbles and Bits with her parents for the time being, since she didn't know if she'd be allowed to stay when she got back to LA.

Finally the two fell into bed to get a few hours of rest. But ten o'clock the next morning found them up and reluctantly getting dressed, because Ava knew Ricky Don would be back at twelve o'clock sharp.

At noon he walked in with a large pizza in one hand and a newspaper tucked under the other arm. After putting the pizza on the dinning room table, he handed the paper to Ava. "I thought you might want to see the front page headlines," he said.

Ava opened the paper and was stunned to read the big bold headline. "CLONEALL DRUGS TO RELEASE NEW DIET DRUG."

"No way!" she exclaimed.

"What?" Lynn asked, coming over to Ava.

"Have you read this?" Ava asked Ricky Don.

"No, I saw it in the paper stand outside the pizza parlor, so I got one."

"Then read it to us," Ava said, handing it back to him.

While Ava and Lynn set out plates, utensils and glasses with ice, Ricky Don read the article about the new pill that promised to "shrink body size by 5 to 10 percent in a year's time, if taken while following a regimented diet and exercising." The drug consisted of a combination of two existing drugs that contained amphetamines and anticonvulsants—and "had some troubling side effects."

The article went on to say that as soon as the FDA approved the drug, it would be available to the public.

"So if a person weighs two hundred pounds and they diet and exercise and take this pill, they can lose from 10 to 20 pounds! Wow! Amazing!" Sarcasm dripped from Ava's lips. "But they'll still be considered overweight. This is just blowing smoke rings up the public's butt! The normal person will read this and think that it's really good news. They won't even stop and think about how brainless it is."

"And the news media will pick it up and start pumping it to the public as if it's the greatest thing since sliced bread," Lynn jumped in.

"Oh, and let's not forget the 'troubling side effects' of the speed and mind-altering drugs that are being used. And these side effects will be read during the T.V. commercials in a soothing voice while the newly thin, finally beautiful young woman skips lightly through the rolling hills with a butterfly flitting alongside her," Ava said. "This makes me so angry I could bite nails! I've got to find those screwed up numbers in that data. I've just got to!

"I'm going to sit at that computer around the clock until I find where and how they changed the data. I have to stop this from happening!"

She threw the piece of pizza she was eating into her plate and started to stand up from the table, but Ricky Don reached out and took her arm. "Ava, sit down and let's discuss our plan."

She tried to pull her arm away from him, but he tightened his grip. "Please. Calm down and let's all three talk about how to move forward."

CHAPTER 10

aTURDAY MORNING FOUND AVA STARING INTENTLY AT THE computer screen. She'd loaded both sets of data onto the computer and had them side-by-side on the screen. She'd looked at them individually, but never together. Maybe by doing this she could see where the numbers had been tampered with.

In the week that Lynn had been back, Ava had found more and more reasons why it made sense for her to be there. Today was a perfect example. Lynn had left early that morning to go shopping, therefore leaving the "watchers" with the impression that the apartment was empty, and Ava could work without the ever-present dread that she was going to get one of their weird phone calls.

As she stared at the data and simultaneously scrolled down each column and each page her eyes became tired, so she closed them for a few moments to rest them. When she opened her eyes they fell on the bottom of the page and scrolled across the screen.

Suddenly her brain came to full attention. The first set of data, the original one, showed 153 pages. The second set read 154 pages.

Clicking to the end of the two documents, Ava discovered that the last page of the 154-page data set wasn't an entire page longer. There was just enough data to feed over a few lines onto the 154th page. That could come from a formatting mishap, she reasoned as she scrolled slowly back through the document. But nothing seemed out of place. No lines were double-spaced that shouldn't have been. Nothing.

She decided to check word count. Bingo! The second set of data contained 150 more words than the original set. But why and where would Professor Lutz have added words? She could understand taking words *away* more than adding them.

Now that she had an idea of what to look for, Ava clicked back to the beginning of each document and started scrolling again. Sooner or later, if words or numbers were added, a word or two would flow over onto the next page on the second document. She just had to check the last page on each document until that feed-over showed up, and she'd be in the general vicinity.

After what seemed like forever, "blood pressure 130/100" flowed over to the next page. Ava glanced at the original document, which hadn't changed pages, and saw "blood pressure 125/80." The data for that research subject had been elevated. The extra digit had tripped the document to the next page.

As Ava focused on the individual numbers of individual research subjects, she found that in the second data set blood pressure numbers had been elevated, cholesterol numbers had been elevated, and blood glucose levels had been elevated. Not for every research subject, but for those who weighed a few more pounds than the rest—and just enough to cause the results of any analyses to imply that carrying a few more pounds than the recommended BMI caused high blood pressure, high cholesterol and diabetes.

The changes were so subtle that the untrained eye would never catch them. Even with Ava's training she wasn't sure she'd have caught them if she hadn't been able to load the two documents side by side on her computer screen and realize that the second document registered a page more than the original because the longer numbers had tripped the end of the document over to another page.

Feeling panicky now that she knew she had the answer, she quickly emailed both sets of data to her password-protected Yahoo! account, knowing full well that she'd already done that. Then she deleted the email from the "sent" file, so if the computer fell into the wrong hands there would be no record of the Yahoo! account. She also made sure she cleaned out the "temporary" file just in case the data had been saved when she uploaded it to the computer.

Having done all she knew to do, she still had an urgency to get the flash drive out of the apartment.

She needed to get it to Ricky Don. But she didn't dare call him. She wasn't supposed to be in the apartment. If Lynn would hurry up and get back, Ava could leave on her bike and take the flash drive to him.

She was too excited to wait for Lynn. She simply had to do something. She transferred copies of the data files to a USB drive, then dressed in her work disguise and stuffed the USB drive inside a fanny pack she strapped around her waist on the inside of her clothes, where nobody could detect it. Then she made her way to her bike, hoping the wrong eyes weren't paying attention to her.

After getting the bike onto the main street and heading toward the LAPD, she began to relax a little. But her brain was still on lockdown. It was almost impossible to conceive that anyone would go to this extent to sell diet drugs. But money was a driving force for some.

She called Lynn and told her she was heading to the LAPD and that she'd reached a breakthrough on the data but couldn't talk about it right now. She'd explain when she got home.

After parking her bike at the LAPD, she tried to casually stroll into the building. She planned on going directly to Ricky Don's desk. But luck wasn't with her. Officer Judy Caldwell spotted her and came in her direction. "Can I help you, sir?" she asked, giving Ava a curious look.

Remembering just in time that she was in disguise, Ava lowered her voice and said, "I'm looking for a Detective Ricky Don McKinzie."

"He's questioning someone. May I help you?"

"I'll just wait, if you don't mind," Ava said.

"It may take a while. He just went in with the suspected perpetrator, and he has two other gentlemen waiting to speak with him," Officer Caldwell said.

"That's okay. I'll wait."

"Suit yourself. Just wait in there," she said, pointing to a room where a couple of other people waited. Ava paid little attention to the other two people other than to know they were both men. Probably the two "gentlemen" Officer Caldwell spoke of.

After getting a cup of coffee from the machine in the corner, Ava sat down to wait. She didn't really care how long it took. She had her answer about the Cloneall Drug data, the USB drive was safely tucked inside her clothing, and she sat in the police department. All was good.

She closed her eyes and concentrated on the changed vital statistics on the second data set. What a huge difference such small changes made on the outcome of the research. How many other sets of data had been tampered with and nobody knew?

"Well, hello! Look who's coming," one of the men said to the other one in a lowered voice.

Ava opened her eyes to see Lynn walking toward her. *Oh, crap!* was her first thought. *But how does this man know Lynn?* was her second thought. She looked at the men more closely. It was the two men in black who had questioned her at the apartment, thinking she was Lynn. Now they were going to question Lynn, and Lynn wouldn't know what they were talking about.

"Well, hello, there! We meet again. Have you found your friend yet?" The man who had talked the most to Ava at the apartment was already up, trying to talk to Lynn before she could get totally into the room.

"Excuse me?" Lynn said, brushing past them and coming to sit down beside Ava.

"Ignore me and play along with them," Ava admonished in a barely audible voice, which only Lynn could hear.

"Don't act like you don't remember us. You and your boyfriend thought you gave us the runaround, but we're on to you now. At least, we're on to him."

"Well, good for you!" Lynn said in her most sarcastic tone. "You boys look like you're up to tackling about anything, don't you? All dressed up like Johnny Cash! Which one of you sings bass?"

"Look, don't be a smart-ass with us. We can cause you a lot of trouble," the second one said, coming over to Lynn and towering over her.

Ava coughed loudly and poured her still-hot coffee into his shoe.

"What the hell is your problem?" he screamed. He brushed frantically at his burning ankle and foot, then stood and drew back his fist as if to hit Ava.

"Sam, settle down!" his partner cautioned, grabbing his arm to stop the blow.

At that point Ava saw Ricky Don making his way to them. "Do we have a problem?" he asked. Ava saw realization dawn on him when he looked around the room.

"Sam Richardson, FBI," Man-in-Black #2 said, flashing a badge. "And this is Tom Lambert," he added, introducing Man-in-Black #1. "We need to have a talk with you and your girlfriend."

"Everybody follow me," Ricky Don said, turning to leave the room.

As Ava got up to follow, Man-in-Black #1 said, "Not you, jerkoff. You stay out here."

"No, jerkoff gets to come, too," Ricky Don said, and shot Ava a slight wink.

"Why?" both men chorused.

"Trust me," Ricky Don said, and walked away.

CHAPTER 11

"**H**OW CAN I HELP YOU BOYS?" RICKY DON ASKED, after everyone was seated around a table in one of the interrogation rooms.

"Well, you do get around, don't you. When we talked with you and Lynn here at the apartment, you didn't mention you were a detective on the LAPD," Tom Lambert said. "That might have helped our cause a lot."

"And you didn't mention you were with the FBI, did you? You might have gotten a lot more cooperation if you had," Ricky Don shot back at him. "Instead you wanted to manhandle Lynn and try to intimidate her into telling you where Ava was. Is that the way the FBI works?"

"Okay. Touché. But maybe it's time we try to communicate and get to the bottom of Mike Campbell's murder. I understand that you were at the Helping Hands institution recently, speaking with Dr. Cochran. So you know about Mike and Mack Campbell. We need to know everything else you know about this case. It's part of a federal investigation, and that takes it out of your hands."

"Like hell it does. When a man gets murdered in my town and someone tries to kill a woman who knew him and trashes her house looking for something, that keeps it right in my hands."

"We've seen the files on your case. There's no proof that the two are connected. But we really need to talk to your friend, Ava." Sam Richardson directed his last statement to Lynn, who kept her eyes carefully trained away from Ava as he continued. "We need to find out what she knew about Mack Campbell, who had stolen his brother's identity. Maybe she can shed a light on where Mack is."

Bingo, thought Ricky Don. The two feds didn't know Mack was still in the area. Which was strange. FBI agents usually did their homework much more thoroughly than this. He gave Ava and Lynn quick warning glances to keep quiet, although neither of them had barely taken a breath the entire time they'd been in the room.

"Who is this?" Sam Richardson said suddenly, as if remembering that Ava was still in the room. "What is he doing in here? This is confidential information."

"Mr. Smith is undercover on this case. He had come in to see me, so he needs to be in on this meeting," Ricky Don assured Sam.

The explanation seemed to satisfy the agent. He gave a slight nod of his head, then turned back to Ricky Don. "So, what else do you have on the case?"

"I thought you said you'd seen the files."

"Well, that was a few days ago. You may have added something since then."

"Nope. What you saw is all there is for now," Ricky Don assured the two agents. *All there is written down*, he thought. And from now on he'd keep his information inside his own head, in case these two decided to come back and check while he wasn't here. "So why are you two looking for Mack Campbell? Why is it a federal case just because his brother drowned?"

"Because he's wanted in Massachusetts for falsifying data,"

Tom Lambert offered. "Working as Mike Campbell at a university there, he 'fixed' some data for a professor who was trying to prove that bipolar drugs have no side effects. The professor pleaded innocent and blamed it all on Mike, but Mike found out what was going on and disappeared. Now they've both disappeared. We think Mike found out that we'd been to the institution. If he did, then he knows that we know he is actually Mack. We suspect he may have killed Mike, hoping that we'd think the Mike Campbell who was wanted by the FBI was dead and we'd disappear into the sunset."

"To be such an intelligent guy, it would be really stupid to murder his brother. Especially if he thought you guys knew he'd stolen Mike's identity," Ricky Don said.

"Well, I don't think he knows we know about that," Sam said. "It seems he'd been blackmailing a former doctor of the institution into keeping Mike a secret. The doctor, William Snyder, recently died of a massive heart attack. We don't think Mack knows that Dr. Snyder is dead. He still thinks his secret is safe and sound."

"Hmm. Very interesting," Ricky Don said. "But it seems you guys know a lot more than we know. I wish we could help you, but I don't think we can add anything to what you have."

"Maybe. Maybe not. Your girlfriend still hasn't offered anything on the subject," Sam said. "Where is your friend? You said she went to be with her family, so where is that? It's not very smart to withhold evidence from the federal government. We know you know where she is, and we have to talk with her."

"She doesn't have to tell you anything," Ricky Don cut in sharply. "Now you two boys need to go on and take care of federal business and let me do my job here."

"We're not done yet. I can assure you we'll be back." As the two left the room, Sam Richardson stopped in front of Ava and said, "You'd better be glad you're working on this case. But even if you are on our side, if you ever do something stupid like pouring hot coffee on me again, I'll take you down. Got that?"

By now Ava's coffee cup was empty, but she made a motion of tossing its contents at him and he lurched backward to avoid contact.

"Yeah, I got it," Ava said in her best man's voice.

Fury turned his face scarlet and he started back toward her, but Tom caught his arm and led him through the door.

"That wasn't smart. Funny, but not smart," Ricky Don admonished. "We don't need them to become our enemies. Until this is over we need them to think we're on their side, so maybe they'll leave us alone."

"I know, but I acted on impulse. I don't like the man at all. I think he has sleazeball potential, even if he does work for the federal government," Ava said, not using her man's voice.

"You have such a sexy voice for a man!" Ricky Don said. But before Ava could answer, he continued, "Why don't we go to my office. That way I can scowl back at all the eyes I can feel lookin' through that two-way mirror. I know curiosity is getting' the best of them. They want to know who my big burly friend is, I'm sure."

After settling in his office, Ricky Don said, "Ava, I went over to your house this mornin', just to look around some more. Apparently someone else has had the same idea. I could tell things weren't in the same place we left them when we found Mike's phone number. So someone is still lookin' for somethin'. Probably the data."

"Do you think kids may have gone inside out of curiosity?" Ava asked.

"I thought about that, and it's a possibility, but my gut tells me the bad boys are still tryin' to locate the information they want. You do have it well hidden at Lynn's, don't you? It wouldn't surprise me if they decided to break in the apartment when they know you're gone.

"By the way, why are you two here?" he asked, as if just now realizing the two women had no reason to be there.

"First, yes, the data files are in a safe place. And they're about to be in a safer place, because I'm giving them to you to keep," Ava said. She reached inside her coveralls, under the pillow that created her midriff, and worked her way into the waist pack. Her hand finally came out with the USB drive, which she gave to Ricky Don.

"This is an excellent idea," Ricky Don said. "But how are you goin' to look for the changed data if I have the USB drive? Are you goin' to move in with me and let Lynn have her apartment back?"

Even though Ava felt a hot flush cover her body at his suggestion, she couldn't resist the thought that flashed through her mind. "Sure, darlin'," she said, moving over to him. "Why don't you give me a kiss right here, where all your ex-girlfriends can watch." She leaned down and kissed his forehead.

Ricky Don wasn't the least bit embarrassed to be kissed by what looked like a mountaineer. Instead he grinned that breath-taking grin of his and reached out and patted her butt. "Come sit in my lap and I'll give you a real kiss, right here in front of the entire office."

"I believe you're just crazy enough to do that," Ava said, hurriedly moving back to the safety of her chair. "I found the tampered data," she said.

"What?" Ricky Don and Lynn asked at the same time.

"This morning I was again trying to find what was different about the two data sets, then I realized that if you load them onto the computer screen side by side, the new and revised set is a page longer than the original."

"What does that mean?" Ricky Don asked.

So Ava explained how Professor Lutz—or someone—had gone through and increased vital numbers, causing the data to show that being over a certain weight was associated with higher levels of blood pressure, cholesterol, and blood glucose levels, therefore implying a higher risk of heart attacks, stroke and diabetes.

"So someone deliberately falsified data just to sell drugs?" Lynn asked.

"Yes. It looks just that way. And they've almost succeeded. The recent article in the paper shows how close they are to getting the drug approved. That's why I've got to stop them. And I have the proof to do it, right here."

"So how are you going to do that?" Lynn asked.

"I'm taking a copy of the information to the local TV station. I want this to be the 'late breaking news.'"

"Not yet," Ricky Don surprised her by saying.

"Why not? I've got the proof right here. Why would we wait to take these people down? That way we can be rid of whoever is watching the apartment, and I can get back to my own house."

"It's not quite that simple," Ricky Don said, glancing around as if he were about to share a huge secret. Then thinking better of it, he said, "Why don't we meet at Just Like Grandma's. I think we can talk more freely there."

"But I don't understand," Lynn said, again. "We're in a police department. What could be safer than that?"

"Even police departments sometimes have ears," Ricky Don said, leading them from the room.

AFTER BEING SEATED IN THE SMALL COFFEE SHOP AND ordering coffee, Ricky Don said, "We can't blow the whistle on Cloneall Drugs yet. I didn't let on, but I knew the FBI was lookin' for Mack Campbell because of the data fraud in Massachusetts. I think we need to wait until they find him, then we can throw in the information about the same thing happenin' at Cloneall Drugs. That will add to his charges when they put him away, and it will also make things go much worse for Professor Lutz. Much, much worse."

"Why do you say that?" Ava asked.

"Because Professor Lutz also knows about the Massachusetts situation. I'm sure that's why he brought Mack in to Cloneall Drugs to do his dirty work."

"But Mi—Mack was in the lab with me the day we both realized the database had been changed," Ava said. "He was as surprised as I was."

"Or maybe he just wanted you to think he was surprised."

"I don't understand."

"I'm not sure why they let you see the first database, unless they thought it was going to say what they wanted it to say. Maybe they were as surprised to see the first set of results as you were to see the second set.

"But I do know that Lutz was aware of Mack Campbell's abilities."

"How can you be so sure? Have you been holding out more information on me?"

"Professor Lutz is Mike and Mack Campbell's father."

CHAPTER 12

As the two women stared unbelievingly at Ricky Don, he continued. "It seems that Mack had been searchin' for his father for several years. He followed a trail to Massachusetts and found him workin' as a professor at Snelley University, the research and development university where the other data had been tampered with."

"Was it Professor Lutz who was tampering with that research, also?" Ava asked.

"It may have been. Accordin' to my source, the professor who was charged declares he's innocent."

"Ricky Don, how long have you known all this? How long have you been keeping information from me?"

"When you found the phone number in your house and called it and said someone who sounded like Mike answered, I started wonderin' about a possible twin.

"I did a Google search on the phone number and found the address for Mack Campbell. I watched his house and saw someone come out who looked like the person you identified at the morgue. I followed him and he drove directly to Cloneall Drugs, Inc. That's the day you saw me there. Incidentally, Mike didn't live in a cheap apartment. It's relatively upscale.

"Anyway, after that, I started doin' a search for Mike and Mack Campbell. It led me to the institution and from there, with a lot of help from the head director, I traced Mike Campbell to Massachusetts. I called the university and asked for Mike Campbell and, luckily, wound up speakin' with someone who was more than willin' to share information with me. Probably a lot more information than she was supposed to share, but she said she adored my Southern accent."

The smug smile he gave Ava made her want to kick his shin under the table. She was also surprisingly mortified to find a tinge of irritation at the fact that some Yankee liked his Southern accent enough to give him so much information. They did need the information, so she'd have to let it pass. Like what choice did she have, she reminded herself. "But why would she share that kind of information with a total stranger just because she liked his country bumpkin accent?"

"Ava! That's just mean," Lynn said.

"Awww, she's just jealous, Lynn," Ricky Don said. "But the truth is, seems that Lola was in love with Mike Campbell and he broke her heart. So she was willin' to tell me everything he'd shared with her."

"So that's why you want to wait and hang them together," Ava said.

"Yep! Both of them are crooked. Like father, like son."

AS THE THREE MADE THEIR WAY TO THEIR PARKED VEHICLES, Ricky Don said, "Oh, Ava, I meant to ask you somethin'. We're having the Fundraiser Gala next week, and I want you to go with me."

"I don't do galas, Ricky Dick. Nobody's, no time, nowhere," Ava tossed back as she swung onto her bike. As the motor roared into action Ricky Don made his way toward her with a gleam in his eyes.

"You wouldn't dare," she shouted over the engine's roar. But she knew he was secure enough in his manhood that he really would kiss her, man's garb and all, right on the public street. So she shot the gas to the hog and roared passed him with a triumphant laugh.

She had to get to work. Maybe tonight the door to the lab would be open and she could get inside. The smile lingered on her face as she dodged in and out of LA traffic.

The Cloneall Drug, Inc. building loomed into sight, reigning tall over the other office buildings in the area. The building was predominantly glass and reflected images like a huge mirror. As Ava approached she could see reflections of blue sky with soft billowing clouds drifting across the sides of the building. It gave an eerie illusion of the building rising out of the clouds.

Sadness engulfed Ava. She'd loved working at Cloneall Drugs, Inc. before she'd found out how corrupt they were. She'd been overwhelmed with pride every time she drove up to this building. Proud to be a part of such a beautiful setting. Proud that her career was being made at such a well-known facility.

How quickly things change, she thought as she parked her bike and headed inside.

She rounded the corner of the corridor leading to the suite where the lab was and screeched to a halt. The two FBI agents that had been at the police department were talking with Carlotta. Knowing they would recognize her, Ava ducked into the closest ladies' room to wait until they were gone. Glancing in the mirror, she remembered that she was dressed like a man. *Oh, crap!* She darted into the handicapped stall just as she heard the outer door opening.

"So how's little Johnny?" a familiar voice asked someone who had come into the bathroom with her.

"He still has a runny nose, but he seems better," the other voice answered.

Oh, this just keeps getting better and better, Ava thought, as she realized the two women were coworkers who had come in to clean up the bathroom. They thought Ava was a man and would freak out if they found her in the women's bathroom.

"How long will you be, ma'am?" It sounded like the one named Linda.

"Could you ask Carlotta to come in here, please? I really need to talk with her," Ava said, trying to sound like an upset woman.

"She's talking with someone," Linda said.

"Could you ask her to come in here when she's not talking with someone?" Ava insisted.

"Okay, I'll check and see if she's finished."

In a few minutes, Linda was back. "She'll be here in a minute. Are you okay?"

"No, not really," Ava answered.

"Who needs me?" Carlotta asked impatiently a moment later.

"Can I speak to you alone?" Ava asked.

"These ladies work for me. You can talk in front of them," Carlotta said.

"I have to tell you something about Mr. Smith. Alone," Ava said.

"Okay, you two go clean the men's room for now. You can come back to this one later," Carlotta directed the two waiting women.

Ava heard the door closing and peeked out of the stall.

"All's clear," Carlotta said, and almost choked when Ava stepped out of the stall. Then she went into a peal of laughter. "Oh, Ava, you got caught in a snap, didn't you? You forgot which bathroom to go into, girlfriend."

"Well, kind of. I saw you talking to those two FBI agents and ducked in here to hide. This was the closest place."

"How do you know who they are?"

"They tried to question me once before. They thought I was Lynn," Ava hedged. "What did they want?"

"They were asking me when Professor Lutz was in the lab. They said they'd been by several times but he was never here."

"Well, he's probably here, just hiding out," Ava said. "Okay, if you'll check to see if the coast is clear, we can get back to work." The less Carlotta knew about this case, the safer she'd be.

Carlotta took the hint and checked the hallway to see if it was safe for Ava to slip out of the bathroom.

They were approaching the cleaning cart and equipment when Professor Lutz came out of the lab with Mack close behind him.

"What were those guys asking you?" he stormed at Carlotta.

"They wanted to know if you were here," she answered.

"Who is this?" he demanded, as his attention focused on Ava.

"This is Mr. Smith. He's part of my cleaning crew."

"Doesn't look like someone who would clean toilets," Mack spoke up. They talked about Ava as if she wasn't there, all the time staring at her as if she were some kind of aberration.

"He's handicapped," Carlotta spoke up. "He used to be a disc jockey, but he was in an accident that left him deaf, so it's pretty hard to do that now."

"But I've seen him wearing a headset," Professor Lutz said.

"Wears them so people will leave him alone and not try to talk to him," Carlotta said, not missing a beat.

Damn! She's good, Ava thought. Improvising seemed to be Carlotta's stronghold.

"So what did you tell those two busybodies who were snooping around?"

"I told them that I didn't know if you were here or not, but if your door was locked and you didn't answer their knock, chances were you weren't here."

"Okay. That's good. You're smarter than you look," he said, and turned and went back into the lab with Mack close on his heels. Just before the door closed Mack turned and looked Ava directly in the eyes, with a slightly puzzled look in his.

"He thinks he knows you, Ava. I could tell by the way he was watching you when Lutz and I were talking."

"I know. I felt him staring at me."

"Let's go clean the bathroom. I need to talk with you without feeling like I'm being watched."

Once inside the women's bathroom, Carlotta continued. "How did Lutz know those two men were talking to me if they were in the lab with the door locked?"

"My question, exactly," Ava said. "And how did they know I'd been wearing a headset? They have a way to see what's going on out in the hallway. I'll bet they have some kind of surveillance camera set up so they can watch everything that goes on outside the lab.

"I wonder if they have the whole place bugged? Maybe they can also hear what's being said in the hallway as well as see," Ava added in a hushed tone, in case even the bathroom was bugged.

"Ava, I don't think you should come back here. I just don't like the way that Mike or Mack or whoever he is was looking at you. I don't want to see you get killed." Carlotta had taken on a hushed voice, following Ava's lead.

"Maybe you have a point. I don't think I need to go into the lab, even if I could find a time when they weren't in there. If they have a camera in the hallway, then I'm sure the lab is bugged, too.

"But Carlotta, promise me you'll get your crew out of here if you start to feel threatened. These guys are dangerous. I should never have come here and tried to get into the lab. They probably have footage of every time I tested the door. I won't be able to stand it if I've put you in danger."

"Now, don't you worry about it. If they saw you testing the door, it only looked like you were trying to clean inside the lab. Go on home, Ava. If I hear or see anything, I'll let you know."

Feeling she was right, Ava gave Carlotta a hug and left the building. She wondered what Carlotta would tell Lutz if he wanted to know where she was, but after seeing her improvise earlier, she didn't have any doubt that Carlotta would come up with something.

In the lab Mack turned to Professor Lutz. "Did you notice anything odd about the hillbilly?" he asked.

"Just the fact that he was odd," Lutz said, plopping down in his plush leather chair.

"I think the hillbilly is Ava," Mack said.

"What? That was a man. How could it be Ava? Is she a cross-dresser?"

"It's the eyes. I've never seen anyone with eyes like Ava. She could make you feel totally loved with just one look, then freeze your ass off with another. This person in the hallway had those eyes. He, if it was a he, was sending you laser beams with his eyes. Didn't you feel it? And he wouldn't even look at me. I'm telling you something was weird about that."

"Well, go out there and get him and let's find out for sure."

Lutz kicked back and waited for Mack to go get the mystery person. He didn't quite know about Mack. He'd been acting a little strange since the whole situation with Mike had taken a bad turn. He might have to make some changes in his plans.

Mack came back into the lab alone. "The cleaning woman said he'd gone home with a headache."

"Did you ask where he lives?"

"I did. She said he's homeless and that we might find him at the local shelter."

"Well, we'll talk to him tomorrow when he comes back to work."

CHAPTER 13

Ava had just eased the bike into the parking place at the apartments when her cell phone rang. Seeing it was Carlotta's number, her heart gave a little jump.

"Hello?"

"Mack wanted to talk with you, Ava. This is not good!" Even though Carlotta was trying to keep her voice low, Ava could still hear the concern.

"What did you tell him?"

"That you went home with a headache. Then he wanted to know your address! I told him you were homeless and to check the local shelter."

At Ava's burst of laughter Carlotta chuckled, but got serious again. "Ava, you can't come back here. And do away with that man's garb. If they see you with that on, they're going to come after you."

"Okay, Carlotta. I'm almost inside the apartment. I'll make sure Mr. Smith disappears. But girl, you are too good! Have you ever thought of acting?"

"Me? Nah. I'd rather clean toilets! Be safe, Ava, but please keep me informed on what's happening. I'm going to worry about you until this is over." And she hung up the phone.

"You here?" Ava called as she came through the back door of the apartment. Lynn didn't answer, and after closer inspection, Ava realized she hadn't come home yet.

She wanted nothing more than to get out of the clothes, get a shower and slip into something more comfortable. She'd had on the uncomfortable costume all day and it was beginning to get on her last nerve.

After stripping off the scratchy garb, she tossed it into the washer. She'd wash it and store it. She might need it again sometime, so she wasn't going to throw it away.

She was just stepping out of the wonderfully relaxing shower when she heard the front door opening. "Is that you, Lynn?" she called.

"Yes, it's me, and Ricky Don is with me, so don't come in the living room in your birthday suit," Lynn answered.

"Oh, that would be okay with me," Ricky Don quickly interjected.

"What's he doing here?" Ava asked, ignoring him.

"We kind of have a surprise for you," Lynn said.

"What kind of surprise?" Ava didn't like the sound of this at all. Lynn and Ricky Don teaming up to surprise her wasn't a good thing.

"You'll find out when you join us in the living room," Lynn answered.

"But I want to know now," Ava said. When there was no answer, she knew Lynn would ignore her until she went to them.

Suddenly not relaxed anymore, Ava hurriedly dressed in a pair of faded jeans and a T'shirt that had seen better days and headed to the living room.

"What have you two been up to?" she asked, then spotted a stack of shopping bags on the floor. "Never mind. I don't think I want to know."

The two people looking back at her wore such smug smiles that Ava's heart rate jumped into full gear. Lynn was sitting on the couch and Ricky Don leaned casually against the kitchen counter, where he'd put a pot of coffee on to brew. Their casual positions contradicted the looks on their faces.

"We went shopping," Ricky Don said.

"The two of you went shopping together?"

"Yep," they answered together.

"So why should this be a surprise for me? Unless it's the fact that it's really weird to think of you shopping together. Y'all got a thing goin' on or somethin'?" she mimicked. "I mean, y'all both bein' from the South and everthang. Y'all probably would fit right in with each other."

"She's really good at this, isn't she," Lynn said.

"She's comin' along," Ricky Don answered.

"We went shopping for you," Lynn said.

"For me? Oh, no. This is even worse than I could have imagined. Why did you go shopping for me, and what did you buy?"

"Well, since you're going to the Fundraiser Gala with Ricky Don—"

"Wait! Wait a minute. I said I wasn't going to the Gala." Ava could feel frustration start. It had been a very long, very trying day, and now she had to deal with this. "I am not going to a fundraising gala. How do I say this to make the two of you understand me? Lynn, you go with him!"

Ricky Don came to her and put his hands on her shoulders. "But I want you to go with me. I like Lynn, but I want you with me that night."

"But why?" Ava simply couldn't grasp why Super-Detective Ricky Don McKinzie wanted to escort her to a fundraising gala. All his coworkers would be there. All those women in the department who swooned over him would see him with her. Did he want them to see him with a fat woman? Isn't that the exact thing that Hank had always shied away from? After all was said and done, he'd only loved her in private, but didn't want his friends to see her. She felt the humiliation all over again, just remembering that last night when she'd told him to leave and never come back.

"Ava, come back to me, sweetheart. Where did you go in that pretty head of yours?" Ricky Don put his hands on each side of her face and forced her to look at him. "I'm seein' a ghost in your eyes. When are you goin' to tell me who hurt you? When are you goin' to accept the fact that I'm not him, whoever the jerk was?"

Gazing into his earnest blue eyes, Ava wanted to believe him. She wanted to let go and just believe that he sincerely wanted to take her to a swanky event and even be seen with her—but she couldn't, and that fact caused tears to fill her eyes.

The tears magnified the hurt in her green eyes, and Ricky Don swore under his breath. "I'd like to kill the sonofabitch who did this to you," he whispered, before taking her lips in a gentle kiss.

"Look, I know you've had a long day, so let's just drop the Gala for tonight," he said, reluctantly dropping his hands from her face. "We can talk about it tomorrow. But Ava, we will talk about it. You can't keep hidin' from love."

"Hank was his name," Ava said. Why not tell him all of it? She was humiliated enough just knowing he'd sensed that a man had hurt her. She might as well get it all out in the open so he would leave her alone about it. If he realized she never meant to let anyone get close to her again, then maybe he'd stop pushing. And who said anything about love? Hiding from love? Whose? Surely he wasn't talking about himself!

"Would you two like for me to go to the bedroom and give you some privacy?" Lynn asked.

"No. You know this story as well as I do, Lynn. It was your shoulder I cried on when it was all over."

Ava walked to the coffee pot and poured a cup, then sat down at the dinette table. When she looked up, Ricky Don and Lynn were joining her.

"I met Hank a little over two years ago," she started. "He was beautiful. If you looked in the dictionary under 'tall, dark and handsome,' a photo of Hank would have been there. When he walked into a room the women literally did a double-take and gazed at him with stars in their eyes. I asked him once if all the attention didn't bother him, and he said that if you were born beautiful you got used to the attention at an early age.

"Anyway, I couldn't understand why he would ever give me a second look, but he insisted that he thought I was sexy and beautiful 'in my own way.'

"He convinced me that he wanted to be with me, so I let him move into my house, which was what he wanted to do.

"But the more we saw of each other, the more I realized that he never took me anywhere where his friends were going to be. He'd talk about parties and functions he'd been to, but he didn't ask me to go to those with him.

"We'd been seeing each other for about a year and I'd finally trusted my heart to him. I told myself I was in love with him, although he'd never told me that he loved me. Then he started saying mean things to me."

"Like what?" Ricky Don asked.

"Oh, just things," Ava hedged.

"Like saying she was fat and needed to go on a diet," Lynn said. "Like saying she'd better be good to him because she'd never find anyone else who would put up with the way she looked. Then he started making all kinds of demands on her."

"Lynn, please," Ava said. "I don't think we have to go into all the dirty details."

"Yes. I think we need to go into every damn dirty detail about this bastard," Ricky Don said. He could feel his anger rising to an unhealthy level. "What kind of demands did he make on you?" he asked, taking Ava's hand in his.

She wanted to crawl under the table and shrivel up into a knot so nobody could see her. She didn't think she could stand this embarrassment.

"Ava? What kind of details?" His voice was so kind, so gentle that Ava almost believed he wasn't capable of hurting her like Hank had. Yet she knew that once the truth was out he wouldn't want anything to do with her. She couldn't believe she'd allowed anyone to treat her like she'd allowed Hank to do. And now she had to talk about it all over again. She could let Lynn tell the story, but she knew she needed to do it.

"During the second year we were together, he became more and more abusive. He'd be so sweet and seductive while we were in bed, and he was a good lover, then afterward he'd tell me that I was fat and ugly. He'd say that he was the only man who would ever be able to stand to look at me.

"I'd make up my mind to leave him, but when I'd tell him I was leaving he'd cry and apologize and tell me he would never say those things again because he thought I was beautiful, and he didn't know why he said those things.

"So of course I'd forgive him until the next time it happened. And it always happened the next time. And it just kept getting worse and worse. He started calling me a whore because I allowed myself to be used like he was doing."

"Ava! You never told me this!" Lynn was horrified.

"I know. The shame was just too much. Then I found out that his company was having a party and he hadn't mentioned it to me. So I decided to crash the party and see what really went on. I found him there with a beautiful, slim blonde and heard him making arrangements to take her 'somewhere so they could be alone.' He never knew I was there, and he didn't come home that night.

"I spent the night crying, but also coming to the realization that I had been a fool and had wasted two years of my life.

"The next afternoon when he came home I told him to pack his clothes and leave. We got into a big fight and he knocked me against the wall."

"Damn him!" Ricky Don exploded.

"Wait," Lynn said. "Wait until you hear what she did."

Now a smile tugged at the corners of Ava's mouth. "Remember the fireplace in my house?" she asked Ricky Don.

"Yes."

"When I fell, I landed beside the fireplace and my hand landed on the fire poker. I stood up, but he didn't know I was holding the fire poker until I hit him in the face with it. Needless to say, his beautiful front teeth had to have extensive work done on them. I think three of them had to be replaced.

"I called the police and when they came and saw my face and the knot on the back of my head, they said he should have had more teeth missing."

CHAPTER 14

As Ava talked, she could feel relief flood through her. She realized she'd wanted to be honest with Ricky Don. She wanted him to know why she could never give her heart to anyone. Ever again. But if she could, she realized now that it would be to him. It would be so easy to love this slow-talking, charming, laid-back, intelligent man who could melt the chrome off of an eighteen-wheel big-rig truck with his twinkling blue eyes and that smile that lit up a room.

"Ava? Hello?" Ava realized Lynn was waving her hands at her, trying to get her attention. "Girl, where did you go? Are you okay?"

Embarrassed that she'd been so lost in her thoughts, Ava said, "I guess I got caught up in the past for a moment."

"Well, that's just what it is," Ricky Don said. "It's the past, so you can move on and forget about it. It's over. Obviously you got mixed up with a low-life, abusive jerk, but let me say again that all men aren't jerks, Ava. And all men don't enjoy makin' women miserable. You've got to stop believin' that."

"I know all men aren't jerks. It's just that I'm not sure I know how to pick one that isn't," Ava said.

"So will you give me a chance? Will you go to the Gala

with me and let me show you how a woman's supposed to be treated?"

"But why? I've seen how women look at you. I saw some of the women in your office basically swooning over you that first day I was at the LAPD. Why aren't you taking one of them to the Gala? You have your choice of a lot of sexy women, but you're insisting that I go with you. I just don't understand it.

"Have you looked at me, Ricky Don? I'm basically a motor-cycle riding, sloppy-dressing Plain Jane. Lynn has told me this hundreds of times. She's basically begged me to have a make-over and change the way I look. But you want to take me to a gala and be seen with a Plain Jane in front of all your cowork-ers? I'm just not buying it."

"Oh-my-goodness!" Lynn said, realization suddenly dawn-ing on her. "In my own way, I've been sending you the same messages that Hank was sending you. That you aren't good enough just the way you are." She came to Ava and wrapped her in a tight hug. "Ava, I'm so sorry. I didn't realize how my words must have made you feel. Please forgive me. I'll never mention a makeover again! I love you just the way you are."

"It's okay, Lynn. I knew you had good intentions. I never felt bad toward you."

"Lynn, could you give us some privacy? I need to address the issues Ava just posed, and it may take some physical dem-onstration for her to believe me," Ricky Don said, a slow smile spreading across his face.

"Well, it's about time!" Lynn said, and disappeared into the bedroom.

Ricky Don took Ava's hand and led her to the sofa, where he sat and pulled her down beside him. He slid his left arm around her shoulders and took her face in his right hand and forced her to look at him.

"I'm goin' to say some things to you, and I want you to sit here and not say a word until I'm finished. Do you think you can do that?" he asked.

"I'll try. But it depends—"

"No. It doesn't depend on anything. You will hear me out. Then if you still don't want anything to do with me, I'll only stay in your life to finish this case, then disappear. But you owe it to me to at least hear what I have to say."

"Okay. I'll listen."

"When I was goin' through puberty, I realized that I wasn't attracted to the girls my age. All my friends would be goin' gaga over some girl and actin' silly, but I couldn't understand what all the hoopla was about. I'd begun to think I was gay, but I wasn't attracted to guys, so I knew better than that. So I decided that maybe I just didn't have what the other guys had when it came to girls. I figured it might come when I got older.

"Then one day when I was in the 9th grade, Ms. Johnson, the English teacher, announced we were gettin' a new student. I was busy doodlin' in my notebook and wasn't payin' much attention, but when she introduced Mary Beth Wilson I glanced up out of curiosity, and there stood Mary Beth with a body that looked a lot like yours. Except yours is better. And at that very moment I got an erection that almost ripped the zipper out of my jeans. Suddenly I understood why I'd never acted like the other guys did. The right girl just hadn't come along.

"Mary Beth Wilson didn't stay at our school very long. Her dad was a military man, so they moved on. But I had a crush on her the entire time she was there. In fact, she was my first love. She never knew it because I was too shy to approach her—" He paused at Ava's look of doubt that he could ever have been shy. "I was painfully shy when I was that age. I was wimpy and skinny, and all the girls went for the football playin' hunks. So even if I had been attracted to one of them, they probably wouldn't have given me the time of day.

"Anyway, I've always been thankful to Mary Beth Wilson for showin' me what kind of woman I was attracted to. And

I've never changed my mind. Sure, I've dated women. I've had relationships with a few, but about the time one of them would start to look good, they'd go on a diet and get skinny. Even when I'd try to tell them they looked better with a little weight on them.

"The day you walked into the LAPD, I was at the coffee machine when I saw you. I had about the same reaction to you that I did to Mary Beth, but I managed to keep everything under control." He grinned at her stunned look. "But I went straight to Chief Jacobs' office and asked for your case, I didn't care what it was.

"I was nervous as hell when I sat down and started talkin' with you, then you started laughin' and I thought you were goin' into hysterics. So you can imagine my chagrin when I realized you were laughin' at me. That hurt me, Ava," he said with mock pain.

Acting on the spur of the moment, Ava reached up and pressed her lips on his. But before he could get into the kiss, she pulled back. "Can you ever forgive me? I'm so sorry I wounded your fragile male ego. But please, I'm not supposed to interrupt you," she said, leaning back from him.

"You're a witch," he said, obviously wanting to continue what she'd started. "But I do want to finish my speech, then we can get on with your apology.

"Over the course of my life, I've never even come close to findin' a woman who stirred my blood like you do. Not even Mary Beth. When I'm in the room with you, you're all I can think about. When I'm not in the room with you, you're all I can think about. Ava, I've got it bad for you. I tried not to get involved because we're warned about gettin' involved with the people connected to our cases, but I haven't been able to resist you.

"So, yes, I want to take you to the Gala. Yes, I want to be seen with you. In fact, I want to show you off to everyone I know. I want them to see what makes my heart pound out of my chest. So will you go with me?"

As he talked, as the honesty shone from his eyes, his words brought a healing to Ava that she'd never expected to have. She believed him. She chose to believe him because she needed to. She'd go to the Gala with him. But she'd watch every move he made, and if he gave her one minute's reason to doubt anything he'd said tonight, she'd never allow him to get close to her again. Even if it broke her heart in half, she'd not let him make a fool of her like Hank had.

"Yes. I'll go with you," she answered.

"YES!" Lynn's voice came from the back bedroom, sending Ava and Ricky Don into peals of laughter.

"She was listenin' to every word we said," Ricky Don said.

"Well, this is a small apartment. And when one puts one's head real close to the door, it's easy to hear," Ava said, wiping tears from her face.

"Are the tears from laughin' or are you cryin'?" Ricky Don asked.

"A little of both, I think," Ava said. "Oh, Ricky Don, I'm so frightened. But I'm so happy at the same time. Please don't hurt me."

"Baby, I'd cut my own heart out before I'd hurt you. You'll know that if you give me time to prove myself."

He took her lips in a kiss that was different than any he'd given her before. The tenderness made Ava's throat ache. She felt love swell in her heart and squeeze out most of the remaining hurt—but not all of the caution.

"Can I come out now?" Lynn called. She sounded like a child who had been sent to her room.

"You know," Ricky Don said, with his lips still brushing Ava's, "We're goin' to have to have more privacy. Would you like to move in with me?"

"I don't even know if you have a home," Ava answered,

thrilling to the intimacy of their lips brushing together as they talked. "I've never seen it. Or been invited to it." She was mortified at her brazen words. Something was happening to her that she'd never experienced. But then, she'd never experienced the true acceptance that Ricky Don seemed to be offering. Was this what it was like to feel so accepted that you felt free to just be yourself?

"Well, we'll have to rectify that little situation," he said. His tongue gently traced the outline of her mouth. "And the sooner the better."

A loud sound came from the bedroom, followed by Lynn's sharp expletive.

"I guess we'd better let her out," Ava said, reluctant to make the first move.

"I guess so. I need to get home, anyway. I have an early case tomorrow. Not that I'm goin' to get any sleep," he said. "You want to come over tonight?"

"Are you kidding? I've got to see my new clothes!" Ava said, standing up from the sofa. "You go home so I can have some girl-talk with Lynn and look at my new stuff!"

"Wow! And I thought I had you almost seduced. You'd give up what I'm offerin' to look at new clothes?" he asked, with his hand over his heart.

"For tonight, but not forever," Ava answered.

The promise in her voice was more than he'd hoped for, and all he needed for tonight.

CHAPTER 15

AVA CAME SLOWLY AWAKE ON THE SOFA THAT HAD BECOME her makeshift bed since Lynn had returned home. Gradually the events of the night before unfolded into her sleep-fogged mind.

Interchangeable waves of fear, apprehension, excitement and mortification engulfed her as she remembered the extent of the night before.

She couldn't believe she'd agreed to go to the Fundraiser Gala with Ricky Don. She couldn't believe she'd gone as far as she had in giving in to her feelings for him, and actually letting him see a glimpse of those feelings.

And she just could *not* believe she'd almost told him that she loved him! Love? She'd never been in love. She'd known all along that she didn't love Hank, and yet he had hurt her terribly. So how much worse would it hurt if she actually loved someone and he rejected her? And besides that, Ricky Don hadn't mentioned the L-word. So she was acting like a teenager with a first crush.

What if he did fall in love with her? She had people trying to kill her. Loving her, at this point, could be very dangerous for him. She could get Ricky Don killed.

No! The very thought struck fear in her heart. She had to discourage him. She had to make him believe she didn't care for him at all. She had to drive him away from her for his own good, she reasoned frantically.

Taking a deep breath, she made her decision. She'd go to the Fundraiser Gala with him because she'd said she would. Then she would find a way to force him away from her.

She heard Lynn stirring in the bedroom and got up to make coffee.

Smiling, she remembered the beautiful dress Lynn had picked out for her to wear to the Gala. Lynn was such a romantic. The dress she'd bought for Ava was totally something Lynn would wear. And something Ava would never have picked out for herself. But when she'd tried it on last night, she realized she looked pretty fine in it!

Yes, she would go to the Gala, and for one night she'd pretend she was beautiful and that she was loved by a handsome, slow-talking, charming man. For one night, she'd be Cinderella.

As Lynn came yawning into the kitchen to get a cup of coffee, Ava made the decision not to tell her about her future plans. Lynn had been so excited that Ava had agreed to go to the Gala and was going to wear the dress she'd bought for her. So why take that from her for now?

The following week passed by without incident. In fact, it was so quiet that Ava was a little worried. The mysterious phone calls had totally stopped. When she left the apartment she still had the feeling she was being watched, but that was the only thing that reminded her that her world was not normal. She was still dressing as Lynn when she went out, so she and Lynn had to take turns leaving the apartment.

Ricky Don had been extremely busy, and too quiet about it. Was he withholding information about the case from her? Or had he seen how much she cared for him and decided to back off? Even though that's what she told herself she wanted, the very thought struck sadness through her heart like a bolt of lightning.

How was she going to get through this? she wondered. How had she allowed herself to get into a worse situation than she'd ever been with Hank? She hadn't missed Hank when they'd broken up. The only emotion she'd felt was the humiliation of knowing she'd allowed herself to be used by an abusive man.

So was that what she was afraid of? Of being humiliated again?

No. This time it would be totally different. Humiliation, she realized, would be the least of her worries. She knew that this time the hurt would be heart-deep, not just hurt pride. And she knew, without the shadow of a doubt, that she was in deep trouble. She was headed for heartbreak.

But she wouldn't think about that now. In a couple of hours Lynn would be fussing around her like a Fairy Godmother, and then Ricky Don would be by to pick her up. Butterflies took wing in the pit of her stomach at the thought of what she was about to do.

SHE DIDN'T RECOGNIZE HERSELF AS SHE STOOD IN FRONT of Lynn's full-length mirror. True to her prediction, Lynn had styled her short dark hair into a look that was sexy, yet fitting for a formal gala.

And the dress—oh, the dress. The pale, lime-green material worked magic with Ava's eyes, enhancing their green color to an ethereal glow. The material of the dress was soft and flowed gently from the waist to mid-calf. The bodice fit snuggly and dipped to a V, exposing more cleavage than Ava was comfortable with, and she kept pulling at it.

"Keep your hands off the dress!" Lynn admonished. "It fits you beautifully! And you can't stretch the material, no matter how much you pull at it. Okay?

"Here, put these on," Lynn continued, handing Ava a pair of emerald earrings.

"No, Lynn. I can't wear those," Ava said, when she saw the earrings that had been Lynn's grandmother's.

"Yes. I want you to wear these and the necklace that goes with them. They'll complete your look. And they're what I had in mind when I bought this dress. Please, Ava. Nana would have loved to see them on you."

"But Lynn, I'm afraid something will happen to them. I couldn't forgive myself if I lost one of them."

"Nothing is going to happen to them. Now relax! Try to enjoy this evening, girlfriend. Can you walk in those shoes?"

"Actually, they're way more comfortable than I ever hoped a pair of heels could be," Ava answered, glancing down at the simple black pumps Lynn had loaned her.

Ava had to admit she kind of enjoyed this dressing up thing. But she wasn't ready to commit that piece of information to Lynn yet, because she wasn't about to totally give up her jeans and T-shirts, either. She'd just have to find a happy medium.

Lynn fastened the necklace behind Ava and stood looking in the mirror at her. "You are so incredibly beautiful, Ava. You shine tonight."

Ava smiled at the reflection of the two friends. "I'm actually forced to agree with you," she said, and they both broke into laughter.

The knocking on the front door interrupted them.

"He's here!" Lynn said. "And you look beautiful. Now go and have a wonderful time! Go. Open the door for him. But I have to see the look on his face," she said, shoving Ava toward the door and following her.

Ava opened the door to a man she barely recognized. Ricky Don had on a tuxedo! Her heart leaped into her throat. The crisp white shirt enhanced his tanned face, and his trademark smile added a touch of macho self-assuredness.

But as he took her in the smile slowly faded, to be replaced by a stunned look. Never had a man looked at Ava like that. Her chest ached with the gratification of it.

He stepped inside and closed the door behind him, still not saying a word. Unhurriedly he lifted his hand to her cheek, then let his fingertips slowly trail down her face onto her neck, then gently trail down her cleavage until the dress stopped them. His voice was rough with emotion when he finally spoke. "You are the most beautiful woman I've ever seen," he whispered. "And this," he said, again tracing her cleavage, "this is the exclamation point to emphasize that beauty."

Ava just knew she was going to hyperventilate. Her breath was coming in short puffs and she simply couldn't find her voice. Thankfully, Lynn came to the rescue.

"Okay, you two! Try to get some dancing done before you go somewhere and get rid of this tension that's been surrounding you ever since the day you met. Go! Get out of my sight. You're making me sick!" Laughing, she pushed them out the door and closed it before the tears came. She'd wanted to see Ava happy for such a long time. If tonight was any indication, she would see that as soon as this Cloneall Drug thing was over.

Ricky Don opened the door of a sleek black Cadillac, and closed the door when Ava was seated. After sitting down on the driver's side, he turned to her. He looked as if he were going to say something, then smiled, shook his head and started the car.

Okay, this is silly, Ava thought. She was acting like a starstruck teenager, for sure. She had to think of something to say. But she *was* star-struck, in a sense. She'd never been speechless in her life.

"I like the car," she finally said. Her voice sounded strained and like someone else.

"I rented it for tonight. I thought the Mustang was a little too sporty for the occasion. And I was right. Ava, you've blown me away. I was with Lynn when she bought that dress.

It looked good on her, so I knew it was going to look good on you. But I had no idea there was that much difference in your bodies!" He shook his head again.

"You know, you men are all alike. If a woman has a nice set of boobs, you don't even know if she has a face or not, because your eyes never get up that high!"

"You're right. But I have looked at your face and I like what I saw. You have beautiful eyes. You have sexy hair. And you have the most kissable lips I've ever seen—or kissed. So Ava, my love, you're a total package! But you never wear clothes that show off all your assets. I'm just a little in awe tonight.

"But don't ever think that it's just your body that has me hooked. I like the way you think, too. You're an intelligent woman. As I said, you are a total package. And tonight I get to show off that package!"

Ava listened to him talk with disbelief flowing through her. Not just her body that had him hooked? Had he actually said that? Words that she'd never heard in all her life. Words that shouldn't make that much difference to her, but somehow they did. Total package? Her? Ava Manning, a total package?

Suddenly she laughed out loud. Exhilaration shot adrenalin through her entire body. Okay, tonight was going to be her night, for real. Was Ricky Don just shooting her a line? So what? She was going to enjoy every minute of it. Just tonight. Just one night to pretend that she was all he said she was. And she was going to play the game.

"Thank you, Ricky Don," she said. "And I must say that you look like a dashing Prince Charming, yourself. I'm quite taken aback with you, as well. I thought some famous actor had shown up at my door when I opened it."

"So how taken aback are you? We could just skip the Gala and do what Lynn suggested." His eyes were on her more than they were on the streets that he was navigating to get to the party.

"Oh, no. I have to be seen tonight. You and Lynn have pumped up my ego to the point that I have to go somewhere and strut my stuff!"

"Well, baby, you have some stuff to strut, let me assure you. And here we are, so get ready to strut. I'm goin' to enjoy watchin' the eyes bulge out of all my coworkers when we show up!"

"But you'll have to introduce me as Lynn tonight. We have to remember that Ava is still in hiding," Ava said.

"True. But *I'll* know who you are," he answered. "Let's go have some fun!"

Neither of them saw the black van pull to the curb. They didn't see the men who watched them go into the building.

CHAPTER 16

THE FIRST PERSON THEY SAW WHEN THEY STEPPED INTO the huge ballroom of the municipal building was Judy Caldwell.

"Judy, this is Lynn Burns, Ava's best friend," Ricky Don said.

"Wow! She does look like Ava," Officer Caldwell said. Apparently Ricky Don had laid some groundwork before the Gala. But Ava had only met a few of the officers, so he didn't have to cover too much ground.

Judy Caldwell was a totally different woman when she was out of uniform. She wore a snug fitting black dress and 4 inch spike heels. Her auburn hair, which was usually in a ponytail or pulled back in a bun, was full and curling around her face, which was beautifully made up.

"Yep. Lynn and Ava could pass as twins, that's for sure," Ricky Don said.

"Ricky Don, who do you think you're dealing with? This is me, Judy Caldwell. We've worked together for years, so you should know that I'm more observant than most. Anyone who has ever looked into Ava's eyes *know* when they're looking into Ava's eyes. Now, level with me. What's going on?"

"Okay, we're caught, but I don't need to tell you how important it is to keep this to yourself. If those goons find out that Ava is around, it could mean her death. But her friend Lynn does look enough like Ava to be her twin, so most folks haven't known the difference. Even the sales lady where they shop didn't recognize Ava," Ricky Don said.

"Then she hasn't been paying attention," Judy replied. "And I'm surprised you didn't trust me enough to tell me. That hurts," she continued, almost making her pout believable.

"Well, go get yourself a drink and get over it," Ricky Don said. "Because here comes Detective Johnson."

Judy turned and took time to speak to the detective, then continued to mingle.

After the introductions to Detective Johnson, he and Ricky Don got briefly involved with a case that was about to be settled, so Ava took that time to glance around the room and take it all in.

Since this was a fundraiser for the police department, the uniform colors were subtly blended with the table decorations. Navy blue and white intermingled in napkins that were folded like police caps, and small gold badges rested in the center of the folded napkins.

Every detail was carefully taken care of, and Ava felt a new surge of excitement from just being here.

"Sorry about that," Ricky Don said, and led Ava to the bar. "What would you like to drink?" he asked her.

"Red wine, please," she smiled at the bartender.

"Whoa! Don't be flirtin' with the bartender. Jim's a cheapskate. He won't give you a discount just because you're a beautiful woman," Ricky Don said.

"And how would you know, Detective? You've never brought a woman this beautiful to one of our humble functions," Bartender Jim said.

"Lynn, meet Officer Jim Blackwell. He's simply a police officer, but he gets cocky because he can mix a mean drink, so he gets to play bartender at these functions. Plus he's the biggest flirt on the force, so beware of him," Ricky Don warned. "Jim, this is Lynn Burns."

"Guilty on the first charge. But I place second only to Detective McKinzie in the flirting department. It wouldn't be cool to warn you about him since you're on a date with him, but if he hurts you, just call me," Jim said, handing Ava a napkin with a phone number written on it. Before she could take it, Ricky Don reached for it and put it in his pocket.

Laughing, Jim took Ava's hand and kissed it. "I'm happy to meet you, Lynn. Save a dance for me, okay?"

"Not in your wildest dreams," Ricky Don said, and led Ava to the table where Judy and her date sat.

Several other couples joined them at the table until it was full. It was apparent that Ricky Don was well liked among his coworkers. His amiable banter kept everyone amused.

After announcements were made, awards handed out and a humorous roast to the LAPD Chief of Police was finished, the band started playing, but was suddenly interrupted by the mayor, who had been acting as the master of ceremonies. "Sorry! I almost forgot. Ladies, we have people passing around some hats with folded pieces of paper on them. All the single women take one—only the single women. Honey, put that back!" he jokingly said to his wife. "At some point we're going to have a drawing, and if your number is chosen you'll be auctioned off for a date with the guy with the most money—er, I mean the lucky winner. Now everyone take part and have fun. This is a fundraiser, after all. And we're desperate to raise some money, even if it does mean doing something this corny."

After the applause and laughter had settled down, Ava whispered to Ricky Don, "I'm not drawing a number!"

"Why not? I'll bid on you. That will assure me that I'll get at least one more date. Come on, be a sport. I promise I'll be the winner. Do you think I'd let someone else have a date with my girl? And besides that, look around you at all the women. Your chances of having your number chosen are slim."

"I don't feel good about this, Ricky Don. Really don't feel good."

"Come on, baby. Live a little. Take a chance. It'll be fun if you do get picked. I'd like to see all the guys fightin' over you."

"That's just the point! What if nobody bids on me?"

"Trust me. You will get bids if you get chosen."

A tall policeman walked up with his hat in his hand. He took a slip of folded paper and held it out to Ava. Her heart pounded as she took it. Why was she letting herself be talked into this? she wondered.

"What's your number?" Ricky Don asked.

"I don't want to even look at it," she said, and handed it to him.

"Lucky number 13!" he declared, smiling. "See. You're safe. Nobody's going to call out an unlucky number."

"Okay, does everyone have a number?" the mayor asked.

Ava held her breath as someone walked up to the mayor and held out a bowl of numbers for him to draw from.

"Number 13!" he called out with triumph.

"Oh, no!" Ava whispered.

"Don't worry. I've got you covered. Just go up there and wait for the bidding to start," Ricky Don admonished.

Ava made her way to the stage. She was aware of the applause as she walked. She felt as if she were walking to the guillotine. This was not good. She wanted to turn and run from this dreaded place as fast as she could, but she didn't want to embarrass Ricky Don.

The mayor congratulated her and thanked her for being such a good sport. "Okay, let the bidding begin," he said, pointing to an auctioneer who was to lead the process.

Is this how a cow at the auction barn feels? Ava wondered. She started thinking of ways to make Ricky Don pay for this humiliation. If nobody bid on her except him, he was really going to pay.

The auctioneer opened the bids. "Fifty thousand dollars," a voice from the far corner of the room called.

A united gasp went up, then the room became totally quiet. Ava found the man who'd made the bid, and her heart lurched in her chest and stopped. She looked at Ricky Don and said, "No. No. NO!"

By then the noise in the room had picked up to the point that he couldn't hear her, but he could tell by the panic in her eyes that something was horribly wrong.

"Well, well, well!" someone standing beside Ricky Don said. "That's William Turnball, the CEO of Cloneall Drugs. It was my understanding that he doesn't even like big girls."

Ricky Don didn't hear anything else as he ran toward Ava.

CHAPTER 17

WILLIAM TURNBALL HAD AVA BY THE ARM AND WAS ALL but dragging her from the room, despite her attempts to pull away from him. All his precious time in the gym that he loved to brag about must be working, because he had a strong grip on her arm.

She was about to just sit down on the floor to keep him from taking her wherever it was he was taking her when he stopped long enough to quietly say, "You'll either cooperate or I'll have your parents by morning. I know where they live, and I have men there waiting for me to give the command to bring them to me. Now, you stop struggling and walk as if you want to be with me, or it *will* happen."

Realizing that Turnball thought he had Lynn, Ava nodded her head and walked quietly beside him out of the building. She thought she heard Ricky Don screaming her name just before Turnball handed her over to a couple of guys who had been standing in the shadows of the building. They hustled her toward a black van waiting beside the curb and shoved her roughly into the back of the van. As the door was forcefully closed, she knew it was Ricky Don calling her name and his footsteps chasing the van.

Suddenly someone in the back of the van with her pulled her arms behind her and handcuffed her wrists, then put a blindfold over her eyes.

"You start mouthing off before we want you to and I'll put a gag in your mouth," he promised.

"Can I at least sit up?" Ava asked, and started shuffling around to a sitting position on the floor before he could answer. Since she was already sitting up, he just grunted.

Leaning back to see if she could find something to prop against, her back came in contact with a rough surface that felt like knobs poking her.

"No! You can't lean against that!" the person beside her told her roughly.

"Well, where can I lean back?" Ava asked in a frustrated voice. "Do you expect me to just sit here with no support?"

"Yep! Now shut up! I told you not to talk."

A voice coming through a radio behind her startled her. "You boys got the cargo?" the voice asked.

So that's what the knobs were. She'd leaned back against a two-way radio.

"Got the cargo," guy in the back with her answered.

"Is the cargo cooperating?"

Why were they being so careful not to call her name or refer to her as a person? Were they afraid that someone else might be listening in on their frequency? Well, just in case, "I'm not a damn bag of potatoes!" Ava yelled. "I'm a woman! And my name is Lynn, so address me as such."

"I told you to shut the hell up! Now I'm going to have to gag you if you say one more word."

"Easy," the voice on the other end of the transmission advised. "You forgot to turn the radio off. I'll see you boys at the house after you deliver the cargo." He ended the call with a laugh that sent a chill up Ava's spine. She wasn't sure, but she thought it was Professor Lutz.

Ava could tell when they left the city. Darkness replaced the thin haze of light she could see through the mask that had been put on her eyes, and little by little almost all traffic noise disappeared.

She tried not to panic as she wondered what direction they were headed and where they were taking her.

She knew someone else sat in the back of the van, but she wasn't cramped, so some of the seats had been taken out to make more room. Maybe they'd been watching her at the apartment in this van, since it seemed to be set up with electronics. But why hadn't she ever been able to spot it?

Having her hands cuffed behind her and not having anything to lean back against was causing her back to ache. She was sitting flat on the floor with her legs stretched out in front of her and leaning forward to try to give her back some relief. She didn't know how much longer she could endure this position before she would have to complain whether her companion liked it or not. She really didn't want a gag in her mouth, so she tried to sit still for a little longer. *Just a little longer,* she admonished herself. Surely they wouldn't take her too much farther.

Then she felt the van take a curve and heard the tires crunching on gravel. Whatever road they'd turned off on became very rough, as if they were traveling over rocks.

The van had slowed down to a crawl, but the bumps they hit were jarring Ava around, and not being able to hold on made it impossible to sit up. She wound up lying on her side and had bumped her head on something as she went down.

The hair on the back of her neck pricked. Were they taking her to the desert to kill her? No. They wanted Ava and they thought they had Lynn. This would borrow her some time.

Soon she felt the van stop. Her companion in the back of the van slid the mask from her eyes.

The two front doors of the van opened and slammed shut,

so she knew there were two in the front, but neither of them had said a word. Then the back door slid open and a flashlight shone directly into her eyes.

"Okay, come on out," backseat companion said.

"Get the damn light out of my eyes so I can see what I'm doing," Ava growled.

"My, my, she's a pleasant little thing, isn't she?" a new voice chimed in.

"Shut up, Dopey," a third voice demanded. "You know we're supposed to keep quiet."

Kidnapper #1 was holding the flashlight so she could see how to slide from the van. The exit she made was none too graceful, and by the time she reached the door her dress had worked up to expose her legs to the rough floor of the van. She was sure she was ruining the beautiful new dress Lynn and bought for her.

Finally standing on the ground, she was able to look around a little. There was a full moon, and she could see they were in a cleared spot that almost looked like desert—but not far away she could see a stand of trees. She saw what appeared to be a rundown miner's shack standing, or rather leaning, not too far away, and realized they were leading her in that direction. At least Kidnapper #1 had taken her arm and was leading her toward the shack. The other two were standing back so she couldn't see them.

"Well, you two going to go light the lamp, or just stand there and look stupid?" the guy holding her arm asked.

They hurried ahead and went inside the small building. Soon Ava saw a dim, flickering glow appear in the window. Then the two came out and hurried back to the van.

She was led inside the dingy one-room building, where an oil lamp with a globe covered in black smut was barely putting out enough light to see the surroundings. She was relieved to see a fairly clean interior with a cot in one corner.

Her abductor shoved her toward the cot, and she managed to sit down before she fell down on it.

It was the first time she'd had a chance to look at him. He was young. Probably in his thirties, with well-groomed hair, a clean-shaven face, and glasses that made him look like an English professor.

What the hell? She'd expected pond scum to be manhandling her the way he was, but he looked like a college student or a businessman. And he was dialing a cell phone, which made Ava smile. One question answered. The area had cell reception.

"We're here," she heard him say as he turned away from her. His voice was so low that she couldn't hear anything but an occasional grunt to the person on the other end of the line.

He finally hung up and turned to her. She looked into his clear blue eyes, and the first thing out of her mouth was, "What is a person like you doing wasting your life in a scam like this?"

Surprise registered on his face before he shut down any expression. "Just keep quiet and listen to me. You're going to be here alone tonight. There's nobody even close around here, so don't even try to escape. There are coyotes, bobcats, skunks and even mountain lions that roam around out here at night, so you won't be safe if you leave this shack. But you'll have to go outside if you need to use the bathroom," he finished almost apologetically.

While he talked he removed the handcuffs from her wrists. She got a whiff of nice-smelling aftershave when he leaned over her to take the cuffs off. Again she wondered how he had gotten involved with Turnball and Lutz.

"Are you going to leave me a flashlight in case I do have to go outside?"

"I'm sorry, but my instructions were to leave you with nothing," he answered, and she saw true regret in his eyes.

"Again, why are you messed up in this?" she asked. "You seem way too civilized for this game."

He turned to step outside the door, then stopped. He glanced down at the flashlight in his hand, then back at her. He tossed the flashlight to her and disappeared into the night.

She briefly heard what sounded like voices arguing, then the van started up and drove away.

CHAPTER 18

THE LAMPLIGHT FLICKERED AS IF IT WOULD SMOTHER OUT at any moment. Not that it was putting off enough light to help, anyway. But Ava saw a small matchbox that Mr. Smooth had left beside the lamp. She checked and it was full of matches. So if the lamp went out, she'd at least be able to relight it if she found herself there several nights.

She clicked the flashlight on and looked around the small shack. The sheets on the bed appeared clean. Her captors had even left a folded blanket on the foot of the bed. She checked under and between the sheets to make sure some desert varmint hadn't taken up residence in them. She didn't want to crawl between the sheets with a snake, spider or scorpion.

She checked behind and under the bed and found only dust. Satisfied that she was alone in the small shack, she pulled the rickety door closed and managed to secure it with a flimsy latch that had been rigged to hold the door closed—but which wasn't any good for keeping out someone who wanted to come in.

There were two small, uncovered windows in the shack. Even though they were covered with years of grime, Ava was still uncomfortable with the possibility that someone could see her, so she turned off the flashlight. Taking her cell phone from her right bra cup, where she always kept it, she held it to the lamplight long enough to dial Ricky Don's number, then blew out the flickering flame.

"Hello?" Ricky Don's voice was hesitant.

"It's me," Ava said, weak with relief that the reception sounded strong.

"Ava! Thank God! Where are you?"

"I'm not sure, but somewhere a good way from the city. I'm totally alone in a small shack that looks like it was abandoned by some miner in the 1800s. There's no food or water. So I'm sure they'll be back. Oh, and there's no bathroom. I was warned about all the wild animals that prowl around here, then told that I'd have to go outside if I needed to relieve myself."

"They're tryin' to psych you out so that when they start to question you, you'll talk."

"That's what I figure. They think I'm Lynn and they're going to try and force me to tell them where Ava is."

"Look, I'm at the station. Let's see if we can get a GPS track on your phone and locate you."

"Okay, but don't take too long. I don't want my battery to run down. I may need to call in an emergency!" Ava thought her tongue-in-cheek joke was funny, but Ricky Don didn't see the humor. "Seriously, Ricky Don, I don't want my battery to run down. When we've finished, I'm turning it off to save the battery."

"When we find you, I'll be out there tonight to bring you home," Ricky Don answered. "I'm so sorry I let you get in this situation. I had no idea there would be a rigged drawin'."

"Rigged?"

"Yes, the number 13 was all that was in the hat. The rest of the slips of paper were blank. That's why Charlie handed yours directly to you instead of lettin' you draw it from his hat. He said the mayor had directed him to give you that number."

"So is the mayor in on this?"

"I'm not sure. Maybe somebody just convinced him that this was a joke, but I'm beginnin' to think there is some inside work goin' on around here."

Ava knew they'd been doing a search on her phone while she and Ricky Don talked, but didn't realize it could be done so quickly until he said, "Okay. We've got it! Looks like you're out on Interstate 5, close to Mentryville."

"The ghost town that's in the California State Historic Park?"

"Yep. You're in Santa Clarita Valley, about 35 miles from LA, and from the trace, it looks like you're not that far from Mentryville. I'm on my way. I'll find you."

"No! I don't want you to come out here tonight," Ava said.

"Why not? I know you don't want to spend the night out there alone."

"No, I don't. But I do want to find out what Lutz and Turnball have in mind. So let's let them show their hand. I'll try to get all I can out of them."

"I don't like it. You're taking too big a chance. If these guys killed Mike, they sure won't think twice about killing you."

"I know. But they think I'm Lynn, so I don't believe they'll kill Lynn until they find out where I am. Just give me until tomorrow and let me see what they want."

Reluctantly, Ricky Don agreed, but assured Ava he wasn't going to allow her to take too many chances.

"Oh! Call Lynn and tell her to stay out of sight," Ava reminded him.

"I've already called her. Of course she's beside herself with worry, so I'll call her back and tell her you're okay for now." Ava heard him take a deep breath before he continued. "Ava, I can't lose you now. I've just found you, and I damn well won't lose you."

"We're going to get through this, Ricky Dick. Trust me, I'm

not going anywhere."

"Yeah, you're real brave, aren't you? You'll call me names when I can't get to you," he said, his voice lightening up a little.

"Ricky Dick, I wish above all things that you could get to me right now!" Ava declared. "Now get some sleep. I've got to get off this phone."

Ava turned her phone off and sat in the darkness. Oddly enough, she felt better after finding out where she was. She and Lynn had come out to Mentryville a few years earlier and had gone on a guided tour of the ghost town, which consisted of several old buildings, a horse barn and a dance hall. She was trying to decide if she wanted to lie down on the bed and try to rest, or just sit and stare into the darkness until the sun came up. Either way, she was convinced she wouldn't get any sleep. She just needed to decide which position she wanted to be miserable in. She'd probably try both before the long night was over. She'd checked the time on her phone before she turned it off, and it was barely ten o'clock.

She'd gone to the ladies' room just before the drawing, but knew she'd need to go before the night was over. She decided to wait until she couldn't wait any longer, so that maybe she'd only have to go outside once during the night.

The distant yipping of a band of coyotes disrupted her thoughts. *Like I'm gong out there with them*, she thought. But they sounded far away, so maybe they were just passing through and would be long gone when she needed to relieve herself. She hoped.

She decided to just lie back on the bed and see how it felt. As she reclined, she became aware of the necklace and earrings she had on. Lynn's grandmother's jewelry! Where could she hide it? Surely whoever came out tomorrow wouldn't be thieves. But she couldn't be sure, so she took the earrings and necklace off and stuffed them into her cleavage. Storage was a good perk of having larger breasts. It was uncomfortable, but that was better than having the jewelry out where it could be seen.

The dress wasn't comfortable to lie down in and the jewelry kept poking at her, but eventually Ava's mind drifted to quieter thoughts. She found herself longing for mom. Someone she knew would worry about her if she knew she was in danger. It was a forlorn feeling to be so alone in the world. Sure, she had Lynn, and Lynn's parents had been so kind to her, trying to fill in for a family, but they weren't hers. And tonight, she needed her own. She needed to know she had someone of her own to love and that they loved her back.

Ricky Don came immediately into her mind. Did he really care for her? And if so, could she let go of her past hurt and open her heart to him?

There, in a little deserted shack miles from anything she was familiar with, she realized that she was totally in love with Ricky Don McKinzie.

The coyotes' yipping drifted further away, and without meaning to Ava drifted into a deep sleep thinking of all the things she wanted to tell Ricky Don. Thinking of spending a lifetime with him.

RICKY DON PACED HIS BEDROOM FLOOR. HE HADN'T KNOWN how in love with Ava he was until he'd seen that black van driving away with her in it tonight. He felt like his heart was being ripped out by the roots and dragged along behind the van.

If they hurt her—well, he couldn't even finish that thought. His gut tied in knots at the thought of not having her around.

He had to convince her to marry him. He didn't want to spend the rest of his life without her in it. In fact, he didn't want to spend another day without her in it. He would ask her to marry him as soon as he found her. And if she said no because that SOB Hank had hurt her, he'd find a way to make her say yes. He had to. And he would.

It drove him crazy to think of her out in that shack alone.

She must be frightened out of her mind. She probably wouldn't sleep a wink all night. And neither would he.

Ava came slowly awake to the sounds of birds singing. She had no idea what kind they were, but the sound was much more pleasant than the yipping coyotes from the night before. The night before? What time was it? Had she slept all night? She sprang from the bed and looked out a dingy window. Dawn was just lighting the morning sky. She couldn't believe she'd slept all night.

But—okay. *Now* she had to go! Opening the door, she peered outside to make sure nobody or no thing was close before she darted out. Glancing around, she saw that the cabin butted pretty close to a small mound of dirt, so she went behind the mound and answered nature's call.

As she stood and glanced around in the early light, she became aware of distant sounds. She heard what sounded like interstate traffic. Then she started to recognize faint scents. Automobile exhaust. Food cooking?

She realized that she wasn't far from some form of civilization. If she'd gotten up during the dark of night, she'd probably have been able to see the glow of the lights from a town.

That's why her kidnappers had tried to frighten her from going outside other than to relieve herself. They didn't want her to know how close she was to the interstate and what was probably a small town.

A large lizard scurried past her, reminding her that she wasn't quite in that civilization, herself.

Smiling, she went back inside the shack. Just knowing that other people weren't far away made her feel much better. She could probably walk to where they were, if she knew which direction to go. If she were still here tonight, she'd make sure to go outside and look for signs of light in the sky.

CHAPTER 19

THE SUN WAS JUST BRIGHTENING THE WORLD OUTSIDE when Ava heard a vehicle approaching. She went to one of the dingy windows and peered out.

Professor Lutz and Mack were getting out of a huge Ford F-150 full-size, half-ton pickup truck. They let the tailgate down and lifted a motorcycle out and set it on the ground. Her motorcycle? It sure looked like it. But why?

Before she could pursue that question, she realized that if Mack had recognized her eyes when she was dressed as Mr. Smith, he'd surely recognize her now!

She quickly mussed her hair even more than it was already messed up from the night before. She tried to arrange her hair in a way that she'd never worn it as Ava, but it was hard to re-arrange short curly hair with just her fingers. That was all she could do. She just wouldn't look directly at Mack.

She heard them approaching the door and sat quickly down on the side of the bed.

"Well, good morning," Professor Lutz said, deliberately being more cheerful than she'd ever heard him be in class. "Did you have a good night's rest?"

"Actually, I did very well, considering my accommodations,"

Ava answered.

"Are you ready for some breakfast?" he asked.

"I could use some food," Ava answered. She noticed that Mack clutched a small paper bag.

"Give her breakfast to her," Lutz directed Mack, who pitched the bag to her. She caught the bag and, glancing in it, saw a bottle of water and nothing else.

"See, here's the deal. You don't get any food until you tell us where your friend is. Now, we know Ava is somewhere close, because we found her motorcycle in the parking lot of your apartment complex. And we know Ava wouldn't go anywhere without her bike. See, Mack here— oh, forgive my rudeness. You've never met Mack, have you?

"Mack knew Ava very well. They worked together. And Mack knew Ava well enough to know she wouldn't leave her bike. So we believe she's close, and we also believe you know where she is. So you need to tell us where she is."

"No, I never met Mack," Ava said, glancing briefly in his direction. "Ava talked occasionally about a Mike, but I understand he was found dead on the beach. I don't believe she ever mentioned a Mack."

"Here's the deal." Professor Lutz continued as if Ava hadn't spoken. "I have a couple of friends in Nashville who know exactly where your parents live. These guys are accident-prone. They've been known to *accidentally* hurt folks. You know, unexplained car crashes or house fires or any number of different kinds of accidents like that. I'm sure you don't want anything to happen to your parents, do you, Lynn?"

"No," she whispered, really wanting to hurt this man before her.

"Then you figure out where your loyalties lie by the morning, and I'm sure your parents will be fine."

The two turned to leave, but Lutz turned back to her. "In case you weren't paying attention, we brought Ava's bike to you. We're hoping if she's close enough to discover it's missing, she'll do something stupid and expose herself. Maybe she'll call that cop friend of hers and report it missing. We'll hear about it if she does that. We have friends in high places."

Both men were chuckling to themselves as they left the shack.

What did he mean by "friends in high places?" Was there someone inside the LAPD who was giving them information, like Ricky Don suspected?

Ava went to the window and watched them disappear around a bend of the dusty trail that served as a road to the shack.

After waiting a few more minutes to make sure they weren't coming back, she turned her phone on and called Ricky Don. She noticed that the battery life on her phone was down to two bars.

He answered on the third ring, and she started talking before he could say anything. "Lutz and Mack were just here. They've given me until morning to tell them where Ava is or they're going after Lynn's parents. You've got to get Lynn's parents away from their home, or they're going to hurt them."

"Okay, that can be arranged," Ricky Don said. "But how are you? Did they bring you food? Did you sleep okay?"

"I'm okay. I slept better than I thought I would. But listen—make sure Lynn stays hidden. They think Ava is close because she didn't take her bike with her. They brought it out here. They said maybe she'd report it stolen to her cop friend, and if she did they'd hear about it. So you were right. There must be a snitch at the station."

"But you can get away if you have her bike!"

"I'm sure they fixed it where it won't run," Ava said. "I'll check it when we get off the phone. I'll let you know what I find out."

Ava immediately went to her bike. The tires were full of air and everything looked like it should. They'd even left the keys in the ignition.

Were they that sure Lynn didn't know how to drive a motor-cycle? And were they that sure she wouldn't try it even it she'd never driven one?

Suspicion niggled at the corners of Ava's brain, but in the excitement of having a way of escape she ignored it and started the bike. It sputtered and rumbled into the deep guttural idle she loved.

"Ricky Don," she said as soon as he answered her call. "They left my bike in perfect condition. The tires are fine and there's the same amount of gas in it as it had the last time I drove it. So I'm heading your way!"

"No! Somethin' doesn't feel right about this. Why would they do that? Even a person who had never driven a bike would try it if they were being held hostage. I smell a trap, Ava. Stay put for now.

"Listen, I'm going to see if the chief will send in a helicopter and find you. I'll let you know when I get an answer. Promise me you won't try to drive the bike. Just wait in the shack until you hear from me."

"Okay, but I don't know why I can't just come to you. It seems so much simpler."

"I'm having one of my gut feelings about this, Ava. Please just do as I ask. Wait for me, okay?"

"Okay," she reluctantly agreed.

"Keep your phone on until you hear from me. Do you think you have enough battery life to keep it on for awhile?"

"Yes, the two bars are still showing, so I'm okay for awhile. But hurry every chance you get. Bye."

She quickly shut the motor off and went back inside the shack.

"WELL, IT'S BEEN TWO HOURS AND SHE HASN'T COME YET, SO she must be Lynn," Mack said. "And from the brief things Ava said about Lynn, I'm not surprised. Ava said she's such a diva she wouldn't even know how to straddle a motorcycle, much less start the ignition on one and drive it. But I would have sworn those eyes belonged to Ava. Those two must really look alike. They look as much alike as Mike and I did."

"Don't start thinking about your dead brother, Mack. We did what we had to do. He didn't have any quality of life, so we actually did him a favor.

"But we'd better head back to LA and get busy with plan B. We need to make arrangements to visit Lynn's parents tomorrow."

Mack Campbell nodded agreement to the man beside him, and wondered if he could possibly hate anyone any more.

AVA GLANCED AT HER WATCH FOR WHAT SHE WAS SURE WAS the millionth time since she'd talked with Ricky Don. She opened her phone and saw that her battery life was down to one bar.

Where were they? Was the chief going to let Ricky Don use a helicopter to find her? How would they do that? Could they do a GPS search from the copter?

As she stared at the phone it rang, startling her so badly she almost dropped it. "Hello?" she answered, recognizing Ricky Don's number.

"What kind of truck did they bring your bike in?"

"A Ford F-150 full-size, half-ton," she answered.

"Bingo! We spotted one pullin' out from a small side road, turnin' onto the Pico Canyon service road. Yep! There's a cabin. Step outside and wave if you hear us."

The beautiful sound of a low-flying helicopter spurred Ava from the shack. She waved frantically and watched the pilot set the plane down in a space she wouldn't have believed possible.

No sooner had it touched the ground than Ricky Don jumped from the copter and ran to her, wrapping her tightly in his arms. "I've never been so terrified in my life," he said, kissing her eyes, her face, and finally her lips.

The uppermost thought in Ava's mind was that nobody could fake love and make it feel this real. She felt her heart opening up for the love she'd never expected to have.

Ricky Don felt the change in her kiss and his heart soared. The sun suddenly seemed brighter. The world was a little steadier. The birds' songs thrilled the air a little more clearly.

Reluctantly he pulled back from her, knowing the helicopter pilot was waiting to take them home.

"I want to see where you spent the night," he said. "They may have left some kind of evidence behind."

Ava followed him into the shack and watched him take close inspection of everything in the small room before turning to her. "Where's your phone? And the jewelry you had on last night? Did they take the jewelry?"

Ava reached into her bra and pulled out the phone, then the jewelry. "No, I have them all in my secret hiding place," she said.

Ricky Don's laugh filled the small shack. "I can't wait to explore every nook and corner of that secret hidin' place," he said, fastening the necklace back around her neck and putting the earrings on her ears. "I'm goin' to take my own good time doin' it, too."

Heat flooded Ava as his softly spoken promise filled her senses. That slow Southern drawl she'd once laughed at now had the ability to leave her weak with desires she'd never known existed.

And remembering her realization from the night before, she knew it was too late to guard against her feelings for Ricky Don McKinzie. She was already in love with him, and there was nothing she could do to stop the emotions that inundated her.

When Mack Campbell had gone in search of his father, all he wanted to do was find the man who had abandoned him and Mike when they were just babies.

All he'd wanted to do was find the father he'd always fantasized would take him fishing and take him to ballgames and do all the other fatherly things a young boy wants his dad to do.

He never once dreamed he'd find a monster who would ruin his life. Never once did he dream his dad might as well have said, "Son, you're just what I need to help me embark on a life of fraud, deceit, and corruption, and help me falsify data that will harm people's lives and even lead to the deaths of thousands."

Never once did he dream that he'd sit and watch his own father push Mike out of the yacht they'd rented to have a "father and son" weekend.

But the most horrible of all was that he'd never, ever dreamed that he'd watch Mike, the mentally handicapped brother he'd always loved and tried to protect, slowly sink under the waves of the ocean while he held out his arms to Mack to save him.

Instead, when Mack finally found his father, he found a highly intelligent man who'd used his mom until he'd gotten tired of her, then walked away, leaving her pregnant. He'd found a man who had known that Mack and Mike existed all these years while he, James Lutz, had become a well-paid professor and well-known scientist, and had never tried to lighten the load of Mack's mother or grandparents.

Instead, he'd found a man who didn't want to be found. But when his father realized that Mack had not only inherited his intelligence but had far surpassed him in that Mack had a rare, but true photographic memory, he decided to bring his son into his fold and make good use of him.

Early on in the relationship Mack was happy to have found his father and pleased that his dad wanted to share a life with him after all these years. Even though little warning signs kept popping up, Mack kept them pushed out of his mind until it was too late to back away from his father.

Now he was in too deep. He would have to go down with his father. But one thing Mack knew for sure. His father would go down, because he was going to take him down.

He would not stand by and watch his father do to Ava what he'd done to Mike. And Mack was sure that if his father had to kill Ava to keep her quiet, that's exactly what he'd do.

Yes, he had to stop his father. And he knew just how he had to do it.

CHAPTER 20

AS SOON AS THE HELICOPTER TOUCHED DOWN AT THE LAPD and Ricky Don and the pilot had unloaded and parked Ava's bike in a safe place, Ricky Don led Ava to his Mustang.

"Why don't I drive my bike to Lynn's apartment and you follow me?" she asked.

"Because we're not goin' to Lynn's apartment," he answered, gently directing Ava to sit down in the car. "We're goin' to my place," he continued, sitting down in the driver's seat.

"Why? I need to see Lynn and let her know—"

"She's already at my place and waitin' on us. I called her after we found you, to let her know you're okay."

"Why is she at your place and not at the apartment?"

"I went and got her last night. I was afraid they might break into the apartment and find her and think it was you. Or recognize her and know that they had you instead of her. Either way, you both would have been in more danger if they'd found her."

Ava could feel herself relaxing. Ricky Don had everything under control for now, so she could unwind after the night she'd just spent. "I sure hope your place has a nice hot shower," she said, resting her head on the back of the seat.

"It has a wonderful shower, and I'll be totally happy to help you enjoy it to the fullest. I give a great back scrub."

"That sounds really tempting, but I guess we need to keep up appearances since Lynn will be there," Ava teased back.

"I'd already blocked Lynn out of my mind! She's always gettin' in the way of my plans! She's like havin' a child around," Ricky Don grumbled.

"So how many backs have you scrubbed in your wonderful shower, Ricky Don?" Ava asked.

"I'm just sayin' I know how to give a back scrub," he hedged, glancing over at Ava.

"Um-hmm. I don't even want to know, anyway."

"Jealous?" Ricky Don took her hand in his and kissed the back of it.

"You wish," Ava said, while her insides jolted from his simple act of affection.

"Yep, I do wish. If you were jealous, then I could hope that you cared for me a little."

"Ricky Don, I—"

"*Shhh.* Don't make excuses, Ava. I'm a patient man, and sooner or later you will love me. I plan to make it impossible for you to do otherwise. Plus, we're at my place now, and I know Lynn is eager to see you."

Ava had been aware that they'd been driving through a quieter section in the outlying area of LA, but had been so caught up in her and Ricky Don's conversation that she hadn't paid a lot of attention. Now he was parked in front of a small yet beautiful house that looked like a Swiss chalet. It rested on the side of a small mountain and was surrounded by trees.

"This is yours? It's beautiful! This is a beautiful little oasis." As soon as she stepped from the car she heard the quiet sound of running water and soon discovered a small stream trickling from the side of the mountain, causing a perfect waterfall.

The house was two stories with a gable roof. The outside was made from some kind of natural wood, and large glass windows looked back at her from all around the house. An open porch surrounded the house, while a covered balcony ran across the front side of the top floor. A curved cornice outlined the eaves of the house, trimmed with decorative woodwork. It whispered home, love and peace.

Ricky Don came around the car and placed his arm across her shoulders. "Do you like it?" he asked.

"I'm in awe! I could spend the rest of my life here!" she exclaimed without thinking.

"Then why don't you?"

"AVA!" Lynn shouted as she ran from the house.

"Well, naturally," Ricky Don sighed, and stepped away from Ava as Lynn grabbed her in a tight hug.

"I was so worried about you!" Lynn exclaimed, drawing back and looking at Ava. "When Ricky Don called and said you'd been snatched from the party, I panicked. You've got to tell me all about it!"

"And she will, Lynn. But first I think all Ava wants is a nice shower or bath and some clean clothes," Ricky Don interjected, taking Ava by the arm and leading her up the steps of the house.

As he opened the door, Ava was amazed at the interior of the house. It had an open plan for the first floor. Dark hardwood floors gleamed against white walls.

A staircase lay straight ahead, leading to the second floor. The banisters were the same dark hardwood that covered the floors. Red carpet padded the steps of the staircase.

To the right, the living room windows looked out over the section of yard where the waterfall was coming out of the mountainside. An oversized tan leather sofa and loveseat formed a nook in front of the window. Open bookshelves lined one wall, with a mixture of books and small pieces of interest filling the shelves. In a far corner, close to the bookshelves, was an oversized, inviting recliner with a small table beside it, creating a reading niche.

To the left of the staircase was the dining area, which fed into the large kitchen. The dining room table and chairs were traditional, inviting a room full of people to sit down and enjoy a Thanksgiving or Christmas dinner. Red cushions rested in the chair bottoms and a red tablecloth covered the table.

In the kitchen white cabinets butted against white walls, but the cabinet doors were outlined in the same red that was spattered through the room. Stainless steel appliances waited to be used.

"I just don't know what to say," Ava almost whispered. "This is so beautiful, yet so inviting at the same time. It almost shouts, 'Come! Live in me. Enjoy me!'"

"That's what I had in mind when I designed and built it," Ricky Don said. "Bein' from the South, where hospitality is very important, I wanted to have a home that invited a person in. You've just given me a perfect compliment, Ava. I'm really relieved and happy that you like it."

"You built this yourself?" Ava asked.

"Yep. It took a few years, but it's finally finished."

"And wait until you see the bedrooms!" Lynn joined in. "Especially his. I mean, that bed of his makes you want to jump in it and never leave!

"Well—as a matter of speaking," she finished lamely, realizing how she sounded. "Look, you two finish your tour. I'll make some coffee." And she headed toward the kitchen.

Ava followed Ricky Don up the stairs and walked into an open landing that held another set of plush leather sofas, this time in black. Against the far wall was a huge wide-screen television, which at the moment was featuring a forest scene with a bubbling brook flowing through the trees and the sound of birds singing.

Before she could comment, Ricky Don slid his hands to each side of her face and captured her lips in a kiss that sent molten lava through her veins.

"I've dreamed of having you in my home and kissing you like this ever since the first day I saw you," he whispered, with his lips barely brushing hers. "I've wanted to kiss you here," and he nibbled her earlobes, "and here," and he nibbled each side of her neck, "and here," and he slid his lips down her neck to the beginning of her cleavage. "And here," and again he took her lips in his.

Ava slid her arms around his waist and responded to the kiss. Oh, how she wanted this! It seemed she'd waited all her life to feel like this. Hank had never made her *feel* loved like Ricky Don made her feel. And Hank had never made her ache with desire like she did with Ricky Don.

She didn't realize she was being slowly guided toward one of the bedrooms until she felt Ricky Don reach behind her and open the door.

Reluctantly drawing his lips from hers, he said, "This is my room. And I want nothing, right now, more than I want to lay you down on the bed and finish what we've started, but I know I can't do that—yet. So I'll show you the bathroom and you can get that shower you want." And he closed the door as he left the room.

Ava found herself surrounded with comfort. *Home,* she thought. The dark hardwood floors were here, as seemingly throughout the house. But the walls were off-white here, instead of the pure white downstairs. A navy blue chenille bedspread covered the bed, with a country quilt folded at the foot Navy blue curtains adorned the two huge windows that looked over a deep ravine.

A huge square area rug extended from under half the bed, so he could stand up and walk on something warm until he got to the foot, where a wooden trunk was placed for storage and to sit on to put on his shoes. Photos of miscellaneous nature shots hung on the walls. So was Ricky Don a photographer, too?

When she finally made it to the bathroom, Ava thought she'd truly died and gone to heaven. The room was as large as the bedroom in her home, which suddenly seemed so tiny after being in this one.

The entire wall to her left was lined with a double vanity with granite countertops. A continuous mirror reflecting the beautiful dual lavatories with brass fixtures ran the entire length of the vanity.

In the far corner a whirlpool bath with six large jets invited her to step in and unwind. It was also equipped with a showerhead if she preferred to shower instead of soak in the tub.

On the right side of the room was a closed-in toilet, surrounded by cut glass that was impossible to see through, lending privacy from any companion who might be sharing the bathroom.

Ava couldn't tell if the floor was made of actual stone or if it was tile that looked like stone. But it was beautiful.

Tentatively adjusting all the settings on the tub to where she thought she'd be comfortable, Ava undressed and lowered herself into the semi-hot, gently bubbling water. *Ah, this is pure heaven,* she thought, letting her mind go back to the night she'd just spent. She closed her eyes and wanted desperately to allow herself to doze off. She felt the tension start to drain from her, and just for a moment she did drift into a light sleep.

Then she remembered she didn't have any clean clothes to put on. "Now what?" she said aloud, as she suddenly sat upright. The pleasure of the tub was gone. How was she going to get out of this situation? Did she dare wrap a towel around herself and go to the head of the stairs and call Lynn for help?

She was about to do just that when she heard a light knock on the door, then the door opened.

Ava splashed back into the water and slumped as far under

the churning bubbles as she could. Surely Ricky Don wouldn't just walk in on her.

"Ava?" She heard Lynn's voice. "Where are you? I brought you some clothes."

Overwhelmed with relief, Ava sat up in the tub. "I thought Ricky Don had come back in here," she said.

"So were you planning to drown yourself if he had?" Lynn asked, trying hard not to laugh out loud at Ava's soaked hair.

"Maybe," Ava answered sheepishly.

"Isn't this to die for?" Lynn said, motioning around her. "The other bedroom has a bath just like this one, except the tile and cabinet coloring are a little different. The granite in that one is lighter than this one. I stayed in it for almost an hour last night."

Before Ava could respond, a loud knock sounded on the door. "I hate to interrupt," Ricky Don said from the other side, "but the station just called and they want Ava and me down there ASAP."

CHAPTER 21

AVA QUICKLY DRESSED IN THE EXTRA CHANGE OF CLOTH-
ing Lynn had brought to Ricky Don's for herself when he'd
come after her last night. *Typical Lynn,* Ava thought as she
hurriedly threw on the designer jeans and red silk shirt. Not
bothering to freshen up the makeup that was left over from her
infamous night out, Ava hurried down stairs to join a pacing
Ricky Don.

"Let's go," he said as soon as her feet had reached the last
step.

Settled in his Mustang, Ava asked, "Who wants to see us?"

"The Chief just said some guy had come into the department and demanded to see you and me together, ASAP, and he
wasn't going to leave until he'd talked with us."

Ricky Don made record time getting from his home in the
hills to the office. As they entered, Chief Jacobs was waiting for
them. "He's in this room," he directed.

As Ricky Don and Ava passed the two-way mirror, Ava said,
"Mike?" Then corrected it to "Mack."

"Looks like it," Ricky Don answered, opening the door and
going in.

As soon as Ava walked in, Mack jumped from his chair and

wrapped her in a tight hug.

"Whoa," Ricky Don said, pulling Mack away from Ava.

"Ava, I'm so sorry," Mack said, sitting back in the chair. "I didn't mean to hurt you. I'm so sorry for all of this," he repeated, then put his face in his hands and started weeping.

Judy Caldwell burst through the door without knocking. "Mack, you don't say a word until your lawyer gets here!" she demanded.

"I don't have a lawyer, and I don't want one," Mack said, gaining a little composure.

"Your dad said to tell you to keep your mouth shut until a lawyer gets here. He's making arrangements for one."

"And how did his dad know he was here?" Ricky Don asked in a voice Ava had never heard before. His eyes had turned to cold blue steel.

"I thought Professor Lutz should know," Judy answered, not meeting Ricky Don's eyes.

"So you're the inside snitch." Ricky Don stated, rather than asked. "I knew someone on the inside was leaking information, but I never dreamed it would be you. Why?"

"Because she and my father have had a thing going on ever since I came here," Mack volunteered. "Now, Judy, please leave. I want to speak to Ava and Detective McKinzie alone."

His voice was resigned, now. He was tired of the life that had been forced on him for the past few years, and he was ready to do whatever it took to end the situation.

"Officer Caldwell, I'll see you in my office, *now!*" Chief Jacobs said from his undetected spot in the corner.

Color drained out of her face as Judy Caldwell realized the Chief of Police had been quietly standing in the corner of the room and she hadn't seen him when she came in.

"I'll send someone in with a recorder," the Chief said. "Ricky Don, don't botch this. We want his testimony to be admissible in court."

When the recorder was set up, Ricky Don nodded for Mack to start.

Looking relieved that it was almost over, Mack sat up straight in his chair and started talking. "I don't know how much you've found out, but I'll skim through some of the history, then I'll answer any questions you want to ask."

He proceeded to fill them in on things they'd already found out, but needed on the taped statement. He told them about his and Mike's history and how he'd gone searching for his dad a few years earlier.

Ricky Don interrupted him and asked, "So when you found your dad and worked with him at Snelley University, did you and he tamper with data there?"

"Yes. When Professor Lutz found out that I tested as a genius and had an almost perfect photographic memory, he realized he could use me to remember where weak links in data were stored so we could quickly go back into those areas and apply the numbers that needed to be changed to bring about the desired results.

"When it got ugly in Massachusetts, we were trying to decide where to relocate when William Turnball contacted Professor Lutz, saying that Cloneall Drugs was looking for a professor and drug researcher to look at data that had been gathered to support the launch of a new diet drug. The underlying tone to the entire conversation was that Cloneall Drugs wanted this diet pill at any cost."

"So your father came to Cloneall Drugs with the intention of givin' them what they wanted. He had all the tools he needed in you. They had gathered legitimate research, but if it didn't give the results they were lookin' for, you could fix it. Either way, Cloneall Drugs would have research that supported a multi-billion dollar diet drug," Ricky Don summarized.

"That's correct," Mack said. "I can show you where I changed the numbers on the data."

"I've already found it," Ava spoke up. She'd sat quietly listening to Mack's monotone delivery, and could have cried at the waste of such a good mind.

"You were so good, Ava. I truly hope that after this is all over, your career can be restored. You were the innocent victim in this."

Before Ava could answer, a tall thin man with a Charlie Chan mustache and dark-rimmed glasses came through the door.

"Hold everything right there!" he demanded. "I'm Hampton Singletary the Third, and I'm here to represent this client. Mack Campbell, don't say a word until we've talked." He smacked his briefcase onto the table and snapped it open, taking out a clump of legal forms. "Professor James Lutz has hired me to take care of you. From now on you won't say a word to anyone unless I tell you to say it."

"Professor Lutz may have hired you, but I'm firing you." Mack spoke quietly. "I've already told most of my story, and I plan to answer any questions Detective McKinzie wants to ask. You can tell Professor Lutz that his game is over."

"But I can't allow you to do that. I—"

"You can walk out on your own, or you can be escorted out," Ricky Don advised the comical looking man. "But Mr. Hampton Singletary the Third, you do need to advise Professor Lutz that he shouldn't leave the area. We will need to talk with him, and you can tell him he will definitely need your services."

"Did you kill Mike?" Ricky Don asked after the lawyer had left the room.

"No. Professor Lutz shoved Mike off a boat we'd rented for the weekend. He said he thought the three of us needed a three-day father/son weekend. I saw my brother drown, even as he held his arms up for me to rescue him, and there was nothing I could do." Color drained from his face and tears refilled his eyes at the haunting memory that his photographic recall would never allow to fade, even just a little.

"Why do you call Professor Lutz by his formal title instead of a more personal name?" Ava asked.

"He wouldn't allow it. He didn't want to acknowledge he was our father until he realized he could use me. He said I didn't need to get in the habit of calling him anything other than Professor Lutz because I might forget and call him the wrong thing in the wrong place."

"So he still wasn't openly acknowledgin' you were his son," Ricky Don said.

"No. He never intended to, I'm sure."

"So why did he let me in on the original database with you?" Ava asked.

"That was a mistake. Probably one of a very few he's ever made, other than getting my mother pregnant." Sarcasm dripped from Mack's voice.

"The data had just come in late the night before, and he'd misread it. He thought it said what he wanted it to say. He was jubilant! I hadn't seen it until he showed it to you and me. When I pointed out to him that it said the opposite of what he thought, and he found out you'd seen it, he knew he had to make sure you hadn't made a copy of the original data."

"So he hired someone to break into my house and steal my computer."

"Yes. He took the computer to his house and found where you'd uploaded both sets of data. That's when he knew he had to get your copies of the data back from you and make you change your mind about what you thought you'd seen.

"Mike wasn't supposed to wash up on the shore, but it turned out to Professor Lutz's advantage. He'd just planned for Mike to disappear, hoping you would get frightened and come to him with the info.

"But when Mike washed up on shore and we had the funeral for him, and you still didn't come forward, Professor Lutz knew you probably were planning on going to the authorities.

"Then Judy told him you'd shown up here at the police station and that Detective McKinzie was working with you, so he knew he had to get rid of you, too."

"So who had the phone bugged at Lynn's?" Ava asked.

"Those were some goons Lutz hired off the street. I never saw them. I know he wasn't too happy with their competency."

"So how were they watching the apartment?" Ava asked.

"They had rented a unit directly across from Lynn's. The van was just to throw everyone off. Oh, they've used the van in other circumstances, but they were watching you from an apartment."

"I think this is enough for now, Mack. If what you're telling me is true, and I don't have any reason to doubt you, I'll check with Chief Jacobs regarding what you'll be charged with. I'm sure that as soon as your plea bargain can be worked out you can be out on bail. Probably later today, but you must stay in the area and be available to testify when the FBI closes in on Lutz and Cloneall Drugs. I'll notify the FBI agents that they should bring in all the parties involved.

"Ava, do you want to know anything else from Mack? Do you think it's safe to let him go?"

"No!" Mack exploded before Ava could answer. "You can't let me out until Lutz is behind bars. He'll kill me just like he did Mike. The man has no heart! Please. You have to keep me in jail until he's off the streets." Terror filled his eyes as he pleaded with Ava.

"I think he's right, Ricky Don. I think Lutz will kill him if he has a chance."

"Okay. Let me talk with the Chief. I'll be right back."

After Ricky Don had left the room and Mack started to relax, he looked at Ava and said, "You look really nice today. I don't think I've ever seen you in anything except ratty jeans and a T-shirt."

"Yeah, well, things have changed a little since we've seen each other."

"Like you falling in love with Detective McKinzie?"

"What?"

"With eyes like yours, Ava, you can't hide something like love. Every time you look at him, your eyes turn to jade."

"It was you who made me decide to turn myself in. I couldn't stand the thought of Lutz killing you. I've been half in love with you ever since the first day I saw you in the labs. So last night when he said they'd captured Lynn, and then when I saw you today in that shack, I knew I had to give myself up to save you."

"You knew it was me in the shack?"

"Ava. I'd know you anywhere. We waited for two hours for you to crank your bike and ride out, but you didn't. I could have wept with joy when Lutz finally decided to give up and go home. Then as we were driving off, the helicopter flew over us. I knew then what I had to do."

"So were the guys who kidnapped me the same ones that kept following me and had Lynn's phone bugged?"

"As far as I know."

"Who is the young one? The one who looks like a budding professor himself?"

"That's Peter Turnball."

"William Turnball's son?" Ava asked in astonishment.

"Yep. His dad says he needs to know all the ins and outs of the business," Mack answered.

"So kidnapping is just part of the drug business?"

"There are things about William Turnball that you don't want to know about, Ava. Trust me, when he refers to 'the business,' he isn't just talking about Cloneall Drugs."

"Ohhh," Ava said, nodding her head in understanding, but not asking any more questions. Mack was right. There were some things just not worth knowing.

Just then Ricky Don walked back into the room with a patrolman. "Mack Campbell, you're under arrest for aiding in criminal activities, some of which are yet to be determined," Ricky Don started, then read Mack his Miranda rights.

"Thanks, Detective," Mack said, smiling with relief as the officer led him away.

CHAPTER 22

TWO WEEKS HAD PASSED SINCE MACK HAD TURNED HIM-
self in. During that time James Lutz had been arrested and
charged with the murder of his son Mike. On his denial
that Mack and Mike were his sons, DNA tests had been done
to prove that he was, indeed, their father.

He had also been charged with lying on federal grant ap-
plications and fabricating scientific data on obesity, along with
several other areas of clinical research, while serving on the fac-
ulty of a number of universities. He was charged with present-
ing fraudulent data in lectures and in published papers. He had
used these data to obtain millions of dollars in federal grants.
If proven, this crime could add several years to the sentence he
would get if found guilty of killing Mike.

William Turnball had been charged with soliciting and paying Lutz to produce false data in order to speed up FDA ap-
proval and boost sales of a drug that could have harmed millions of people. Cloneall Drugs' doors had been closed, and
production of all their drugs had been halted until further investigation.

Mack had been charged with aiding, but after a plea bargain
in exchange for his testimony against Lutz and Turnball, he

was free on a three-year probation. He was never to work as a researcher again.

Before deeper investigation could be done on Judy Caldwell, she had quickly left town.

After all guilty parties had been arrested and charged, Ava was free to go back to her home and try to clean up her damaged things. She'd considered hiring someone to come in and do the job, but she wanted to be the one to check everything and decide what she could salvage. And she wanted to be able to say goodbye to all the things she had to throw away. She'd turned down Lynn's offer to help, and Lynn understood her need to be alone to do what had to be done.

Ricky Don was a different matter. At first he'd insisted on staying with her. He just couldn't understand why she needed to be alone with the process. But finally Ava had convinced him it must just be a "woman thing," and he agreed to leave her alone.

Now she glanced around at the progress she'd made. She had tackled the bedrooms first, because the damage there hadn't been as great as it was in the living room. But in the end she wound up washing every item in her bedroom. She couldn't stand the thought of the goons' grubby fingerprints being on anything that went on her body.

Today she'd tackled the living room. She'd held items that had been her mom's that were now so broken they could never be repaired. One vase, in particular, she couldn't bear to let go. It was in several pieces, but even that damaged she could remember how much her mom had loved it. There had always been fresh flowers in it when her mom was alive. So Ava gently wrapped the vase in tissue paper and stored it in a sturdy box.

She was going to have to purchase all new living room furniture. And of course she'd have to have a new computer.

Suddenly, just looking around her and thinking of all the

damage to her keepsakes, all the money these villains would cost her—not to even mention the mental damage she'd been through—made her want to scream. She wanted to hit something—or someone! Preferably the jerks who were safely in jail and out of her reach.

And all of a sudden it just seemed too much to take. Ava sank dejectedly to the floor, buried her face in her hands, and wept.

That's how Ricky Don found her when he walked through the front door.

This is why I didn't want her here alone, he thought, as he sat down beside her and gathered her close.

Ava was so caught up in her distress that she hadn't bothered to be frightened when arms went around her. She knew, even before she smelled his cologne, that it was Ricky Don.

Fighting for control, she turned her tear-streaked face up to him and tried to force a smile. But before the smile developed he captured her lips in his. Her first thought was to resist the kiss, but his lips were playing havoc with her emotions. The anger that she'd felt moments before was being replaced by a different kind of heat that burned through her entire body.

He'd never, ever kissed her like this. Or at least she'd never responded like this, if he had. Every inch of her skin longed to be touched by him, and she longed to touch every inch of him.

Ricky Don felt the change in her. Hope took new roots in his heart. He'd never wanted any woman like he wanted Ava. But he didn't just want to make love with her. He wanted to spend his life making love with her. Making love. Making babies. Making a life together. He wanted to know her, mind, body and soul. He wanted to be one with Ava Manning.

When he finally pulled away from her to look down at her tear-streaked face, he thought he'd never seen a more beautiful face. It was the face he wanted to wake up to every morning for the rest of his life. The face he wanted to see when he came home from a long day at work.

"Will you marry me, Ava?" He saw the surprise leap into her eyes, and knew how she felt. He hadn't come here today planning on proposing to her. He was planning a much more romantic proposal in the next few days, but it had just slipped out.

"But, Ricky Don, we've talked about this—"

"No. You've talked about all the reasons why it won't work. I don't want to hear any more of those reasons. All I want to hear is you tellin' me that you'll spend the rest of your life with me. So, will you?"

Ava looked deeply into the beautiful blue eyes that could make her weak with just one of his small, almost undetected winks when he was sharing a thought with just her. She gazed at his lips, which could smile so easily, yet drain her of all energy when he kissed her. She heard the adorable accent that at one time had sent her into a peal of uncontrollable laughter, but had now become so appealing she didn't want to ever be in a place she couldn't hear it.

But most of all, she thought about the man who held her in his arms and declared that he wanted to spend his life with her. She still couldn't figure out why he wanted her. Why he loved her. She didn't know those answers. But she did know that Ricky Don McKinzie was a good, honorable man. And even more than that, she couldn't imagine a life without him. Didn't want to even think of living without him. So she had to believe it would work. If she didn't try, she'd never know.

"Ricky Dick, I thought you'd never ask!" she said, and went into peals of laughter as he pushed her back on the floor and kissed her until she felt she was going to melt and dissolve into the carpet.

About the Author

PAT BALLARD LIVES IN NASHVILLE, TN. SHE WRITES MOTI-vational romance novels to show that plus-size women can be just as sexy, romantic and exciting as their slim sisters.

Visit Pat on the web at www.patballard.com. Sign up for her free email newsletter, The Queen's Proclamation, at www.pearlsong.com/pat_ballard.htm.

Look for her other books published by Pearlsong Press— *Dangerous Curves Ahead: Short Stories, Wanted: One Groom, Nobody's Perfect, His Brother's Child, A Worthy Heir, Abigail's Revenge* & *The Best Man* in trade paperback or ebook editions at your favorite online bookstore, as well as at www.pearlsong.com.

THE QUEEN OF RUBENESQUE ROMANCES HAS ALSO VENTURED into nonfiction! *10 Steps to Loving Your Body (No Matter What Size You Are)* has been called "your body's best friend in pocket form" and has been named one of the Top 100 Best Self-Help Books of All Time by Self-help.fm. It's also available in trade paperback and ebook editions.

About Pearlsong Press

Pearlsong Press is an independent publishing company dedicated to providing books and resources that entertain while expanding perspectives on the self and the world. The company was founded by Peggy Elam, Ph.D., a psychologist and journalist, in 2003.

Pearls are formed when a piece of sand or grit or other abrasive, annoying, or even dangerous substance enters an oyster and triggers its protective response. The substance is coated with shimmering opalescent nacre ("mother of pearl"), the coats eventually building up to produce a beautiful gem. The self-healing response of the oyster thus transforms suffering into a thing of beauty.

The pearl-creating process reflects our company's desire to move outside a pathological or "disease" based model of life, health and well-being into a more integrative and transcendent perspective. A move out of suffering into joy. And that, we think, is something to sing about.

Pearlsong Press endorses Health At Every Size, an approach to health and well-being that celebrates natural diversity in body size and encourages people to stop focusing on weight (or any external measurement) in favor of listening to and respecting natural appetites for food, drink, sleep, rest, movement, and recreation. While not every book we publish specifically promotes Health At Every Size (by, for instance, featuring fat heroines or educating readers on size acceptance), none of our books or other resources will contradict this holistic and body-positive perspective.

We encourage you to enjoy, enlarge, and enlighten yourself with other Pearlsong Press books, which you can purchase at www.pearlsong.com or your favorite bookstore. Keep up with us through our blog at www.pearlsongpress.com.

Fiction:

The Season of Lost Children—a novel by Karen Blomain
The Fat Lady Sings—a young adult novel by Charlie Lovett

Syd Arthur—a novel by Ellen Frankel
Fallen Embers (Book One of The Embers Series)
—paranormal romance by Lauri J Owen
Bride of the Living Dead—romantic comedy by Lynne Murray
Measure By Measure—a romantic romp with the fabulously fat
by Rebecca Fox & William Sherman
FatLand—a visionary novel by Frannie Zellman
The Program—a suspense novel by Charlie Lovett
The Singing of Swans—a novel about the Divine Feminine
by Mary Saracino

ROMANCE NOVELS & SHORT STORIES
FEATURING BIG BEAUTIFUL HEROINES:

by Pat Ballard, the Queen of Rubenesque Romances—
The Best Man | Abigail's Revenge
Dangerous Curves Ahead: Short Stories | Wanted: One Groom
Nobody's Perfect | His Brother's Child | A Worthy Heir
by Rebecca Brock—*The Giving Season*
& by Judy Bagshaw—*At Long Last, Love: A Collection*

NONFICTION:
Fat Poets Speak: Voices of the Fat Poets' Society
—edited by Frannie Zellman
Ten Steps to Loving Your Body (No Matter What Size You Are)
by Pat Ballard
Beyond Measure: A Memoir About Short Stature & Inner Growth
by Ellen Frankel
Taking Up Space: How Eating Well & Exercising Regularly
Changed My Life by Pattie Thomas, Ph.D. with Carl Wilkerson,
M.B.A. (foreword by Paul Campos, author of *The Obesity Myth*)
Off Kilter: A Woman's Journey to Peace with Scoliosis, Her Mother
& Her Polish Heritage—a memoir by Linda C. Wisniewski
Unconventional Means: The Dream Down Under
—a spiritual travelogue & memoir by Anne Richardson Williams
Splendid Seniors: Great Lives, Great Deeds
—inspirational biographies by Jack Adler

AND MORE!